Changing Time
SERIES

CLEETHORPES AND DISTRICT
remembered

Changing Times
SERIES

CLEETHORPES
AND DISTRICT
remembered

Brian Leonard

TEMPUS

Frontispiece: *A symbol of Cleethorpes – the Leaking Boot – on a Bamforth postcard from the 1950s.*

First published 2003

Tempus Publishing Limited
The Mill, Brimscombe Port,
Stroud, Gloucestershire, GL5 2QG
www.tempus-publishing.com

© Brian Leonard, 2003

British Library Cataloguing in Publication Data.
A catalogue record for this book is available from the British Library.

ISBN 0 7524 3003 3

Typesetting and origination by Tempus Publishing Limited
Printed in Great Britain by Midway Colour Print, Wiltshire

Contents

Acknowledgements

On seeing the book *Grimsby Remembered* several people asked, 'Are you doing Cleethorpes next?' My answer was 'No, definitely not!' However, their persistence has made the book become reality, and has provided a wealth of interesting memories of the area. My thanks go to all those for giving much encouragement, and to David Buxton of Tempus Publishing who agreed to publish this book.

Grateful thanks are extended to the following people for stories and memories, photographs, background information, and for putting me in touch with other contributors:
Michael Allen (Dronfield); Revd Roy Allinson (Devon); Jean Ashling; Mary Bailey (Sheffield); Mary Barker (Sheffield); Marjorie Barron; Mrs E. Barson (Sheffield); John D. Beasley (Peckham); Stephanie Bennett; Arthur Beyless (Leicester); Maureen Boulton (Leicester); David Bradley; Tricia Bradley; Gary Carson; Dorothy Caufield; John Coulam; Simon Drake; Norman Drewry (Hinckley); Ron Driver; Joan East; David Edwards; Alf Evardson; Jim and Pam Everett; Alan Fisher; Edgar Fisher; Keith Ford; Susan Fotheringham; Mrs M. Frost (Sheffield); Sid Fryer; Jack Gibney; Sylvia Grant (Leicester); Tony Griffiths; Barry Hall; Alan Hardwick (of BBC Radio Lincolnshire); Michelle Harris; Pat Harvey (East Goscote); Norman Hastings (Queniborough); John Hewson (Leicester); Enid Hickingbotham (Stouchsburg, United States of America); Lindy Holbrook and staff of Bursar Street School; Carol Hurst (Belper); Ian Jackson; David Jagger; John Kirkby; Lester Kitching; Chris Leonard (Fakenham); Sandra Leonard; Tony Light (Bristol); Beryl Lusby; Richard Lyon; Ivy Maidens; Andy Marsh; Tim Mickleburgh; Tina Miller; Mrs B. Morley (Mountsorrel); George Morton; Iris Morton; Terry Nundy (Cropston); Lynn Padmore (Thurmaston); Margaret Page (Oadby); David and Sue Parr; Doreen Phillips; Ron Pudsey (of *The Lincolnshire and East Yorkshire Transport Review*); Anne Reynolds (Sheffield); Joyce Robinson; Sally Russell (Derby); Jeff Sandford (Cumbria); Roy Shaw; Mr E. Smith; the children of Springfield Primary School; Mike Stevens; Howard Swain; David Thomas; Maureen Thompson; Vera Thorpe; Joyce Tyson; Ralph Walker (Rotherham); Mrs P. Warren (Derby); Doug Wise; Tom Williams (Leicester); Paul Williamson (Leicester) and Ray Woods.

My collection of *Bygones* supplements published by the *Grimsby Telegraph* has been a valuable resource of information in checking details and dates. The *Grimsby Telegraph* has set a creditable example in fostering interest in local history. I am also indebted to the editors of various local and national newspapers who included my letter appealing for information.

I am very grateful to those who allowed me access to their collections of postcards. I have endeavoured to trace the owners of copyright of all photographs used and thank them for granting permission. Unfortunately a few have evaded me. Please accept my apologies if you are omitted. I shall be pleased to include your name in any revision.

Norman Drewry on a bird-watching visit to Humberston salt marshes in 1954-'55. Norman has provided many memories and photographs from when he lived in the area.

Special thanks go to John D. Beasley for giving of his experience in writing, and for reading the original typescript and proofs. Also, special thanks go to David G. Bradley for his enthusiasm in checking details, and his company on our various walks around Cleethorpes. Lastly to my wife, Sandra, thanks for suffering the piles of paper!

A postcard dating from around 1930, of Brighton Street slipway and High Cliff. However, the 2d stamp bears the head of a young George VI.

Introduction

We all know the words of the famous song, adopted by Blackpool as its anthem: *Oh, we do like to be beside the seaside*. As an island nation we enjoy the sea, and those who are not sailors enjoy the coastal resorts. For many people, being, or living, beside the seaside is not an option. We were born here. Our childhood memories are centred here. Our roots are here. So the best people to ask about Cleethorpes' history – its living history, that is – are the people who have lived here all their lives. That is where this book started, but the influence of Cleethorpes has been found to stretch much further.

Casual visitors to the town have memories of their weeks, days, or sometimes only hours here, and an outsider's viewpoint can be more objective than that of a resident. Thus I invited Cleethorpes' visitors from all over the country to contribute to this compilation. Many people in the Midlands have vivid memories of holidays in this area, when their town closed for its annual week's holiday, and residents came to Cleethorpes in their thousands. Indeed, some weeks in July and August were known by the name of the town or city that visited. Other anecdotes have come from far and wide as Cleethorpes' residents have moved away. One reminiscence and photograph even crossed the Atlantic!

However, Cleethorpes is not just a seaside resort. It is also a shopping centre, a workplace, and sometimes a place of sadness. All of these aspects of life are reflected in this book.

As with any town, Cleethorpes is a centre of influence in the surrounding area. Few towns can survive without the collection of villages, farms and industries around them. So I have invited people from the district to contribute memories, too.

For many people, the symbol of Cleethorpes is the 'Boy with the Leaking Boot'. Jim Everett tells how his father, employed by Cleethorpes Borough Council as foreman, signwriter and painter, often had to refurbish the statue as a result of vandalism. On one occasion after repairs, and to deter further damage, his father hit on the idea of liberally coating the statue with a mixture of axle/wagon grease and gold gloss paint. Whether the trial was a success, Jim cannot remember, as the statue was stolen or wrecked soon after. But the symbol continues, albeit in fibreglass now.

One of my own distant memories of the area is the tin mission chapel that had been sited near to Great Coates railway station. It had been built in 1900, but was moved in 1945 to Garden Street, Grimsby, to replace a similar one bombed a few months before. The only picture of the building I have found is on page 4 of *The Railways around Grimsby, Cleethorpes, Immingham and North East Lincolnshire* by Paul King and Dave Hewins, where the chapel nestles behind Garden

Street signal box. Is there a photograph of the chapel in its original position at Great Coates?

I received this kind tribute from Jean Ashling:

> What great pleasure Brian is giving to so many people through his books. Not only to the readers but also to those who contribute by supplying photos and memories.
>
> We are continually exhorted to 'look to the future', 'build for the future' and 'save for the future'. Whilst no one disputes the wisdom of these words, it is equally important to look back to the past. Life is continuous – not compartmentalised into past, present and future. For many of us researching for Brian's book, the journeying has evoked many memories that would have otherwise lain dormant in our subconscious. Brian has been instrumental in helping us to recapture many happy and interesting episodes in our lives. Our 'present' is founded on 'yesterday's future'.

I hope that you enjoy looking back at the past, and that perhaps you discover something new and interesting.

1 Home Life

Meggies, and proud of it!

It wasn't unusual for us to walk out to Haile Sand Fort, following the receding tide, and then hurrying back before the tide turned. It was a dangerous practice but we didn't realise it at the time. We were Meggies, born over Isaac's Hill, and this was OUR place where we could come to no harm. Meggies were once called 'red flannelites' too. The old story says that one night a sailing ship with a hold full of red flannel ran aground on Cleethorpes' sand. The result was that every woman in Cleethorpes – little more than a village at the time – wore red flannel petticoats and unmentionables for years afterwards!

Iris Morton

Humberside – an Improvement for the people?

When he was eighty-two, my father felt the time was 'right' and began clearing out his belongings. He came across his medals and some documents from the two world wars. There was a box of photographs too, of him in the army and of his family in Cleethorpes years ago. I wasn't all that interested in old things then, so he decided he would leave them to the town for future generations to enjoy. He rang the public library and was given the phone number of the new Humberside museum service. He was surprised that it was a Hull number but he rang it anyway.

The person who answered declared that they 'would be delighted' to have Dad's items. Dad asked about them being available to Cleethorpes people, and the answer made him very cross. The impression he was given was that these items of Cleethorpes' interest would be stored in the archives (in Hull or Beverley) until such time as they 'could get round to them', and even then there was no guarantee that they would ever be displayed in Cleethorpes. 'Everything is done at county level now,' was one comment.

Dad was upset and far from impressed by this overbearing attitude. 'Hull is taking us over!' he declared.

He died a year later and we never found those medals and photographs. I think he threw them away rather than have them lost in Hull or Beverley. I wish I had taken more interest in them.

When it was proposed that the biased Humberside authority be abolished, I was all for it.

Tina Miller

Much has changed

As a child in the early 1950s my parents (who helped at the Bethel Mission Sunday School) and I used to travel on a bus from Yarborough Road, Grimsby, to Fiveways, which is on the border of Grimsby and Cleethorpes. Then we had to walk to the Bethel Mission in Tiverton Street on the corner of Harrington Street, to

St Peter's Road (now Avenue!) and Wesleyan chapel, Cleethorpes. This postcard is dated 27 March 1909, and the message to 'Miss A. Russell of 62 Earl Street, Local' reads, 'Weather permitting we are all improving, Love, Nell.'

go to the Sunday school which was held there. I attended for many years and had an enjoyable time.

For the Sunday school anniversary a temporary stage was constructed using wooden fish boxes borrowed from the Grimsby Fish Docks and arranged at different heights. This was done so that we could be seen by the congregation. What wonderful times we had, singing and reciting. We were dressed in our Sunday best.

The Port Missioner was a very good friend of my parents. We stayed for tea with him and his family because it took too long to go home and get back in time for each service.

My parents would sometimes take me onto Cleethorpes front for a walk after Sunday school had finished. One day I asked if I could have an ice cream and my daddy said, 'No, it is the Lord's day and we do not buy from ice cream parlours on His day.' I did not really understand until later on in years. Times have changed very much since then.

Tricia Bradley

Friday 22 November 1963

What were you doing when President Kennedy was assassinated? The question, and the memories and situations that it evokes, fascinate many people. We all have our story to tell.

I was waiting on the platform at King's Cross station for the train bringing my fiancée from Cleethorpes to visit me at college. She told me she had seen the newspaper placards at Peterborough, and the passengers in her compartment had started to speak to each other in a most un-British way. All their national reserve had left them as they discussed the event.

At King's Cross, I heard the news with disbelief, that one so young, so prominent, and seemingly so well-liked as JFK, could be the victim of such a cowardly act of terrorism. Sadly it was true.

Gary Carson

The town fire brigade

My father, Charlie Humberstone, retired from the Cleethorpes fire brigade in 1945 after twenty-six years' service. He was the reserve driver, after Snowy Hopkinson, who lived in

Poplar Road opposite the fire station. If either of them left Cleethorpes they let the other know, even if they were going only as far as Grimsby. One always stayed in Cleethorpes.

The main fires in Cleethorpes, especially in the Dolphin and Cuttleby areas, were fishermen's house fires. These inshore fishermen used to put their nets into the copper to boil with the tar to cover them. The tar would boil over onto the floor, catch alight and set fire to everything around. The houses in these streets had false roofs which were all joined so fire soon spread.

About 1936 all the firemen's houses were issued with a bell. We lived in Bennett Road and every night at 5.30 p.m. the bell was tested. If we had our front door open, the bell could be heard at the end of Pelham Road and Chapman Road.

About once or twice a month, Pop would stay behind after work at the council yard in Poplar Road and call in at the fire station to

Cleethorpes' Dennis fire engine in around 1922. Charlie Humberstone is the only fireman not sporting the fashionable moustache.

Official photograph of the officers of Cleethorpes fire station in 1939. From left to right, back row are Charlie Butler, Len Draper, Jack Garnet, ? Harvey, Charlie Rowntree, Charlie Robinson and Steve Charlton. Middle row: Snowy Hopkinson (driver), Jack Philipson, ? Cook, ? Bell (Fire Chief), ? Yeardley, Jock Gray, and Charlie Humberstone. Front row: Jack Todd, ? Lazarus, Jack Westerman, -?-.

give the engine and the bell a polish. My friend, Lorna Marshall, who lived at 11 Bennett Road, and I would go to 'help' him. We enjoyed ringing the bell on the engine. The new engine came in 1938. An official presentation was held one afternoon and Mam was invited. She sat on a seat opposite the station.

When the war came, the old Dennis fire engine was used to cover the top end of Cleethorpes (Queens Parade area). Pop drove it to the Blue Bird garage on Taylor's Avenue. Snowy Hopkinson covered the Grimsby end of Cleethorpes, which all worked very well. When the Auxiliary Fire Service was formed, and then became the National Fire Service, Pop was a retained fireman. He agreed to cover most Sundays, but insisted on having two off: Beaconthorpe Methodist Men's Weekend and

Harvest Festival. Sometimes the air-raid siren sounded six times in the night. Pop attended every one of them and worked every day as well. He never missed anything. There was no stress counselling available in those days!

Joyce Tyson

Watching every penny

My wife recalls having to alight with her mother from the tram at the bottom of Isaac's Hill and walk up to their home at the top of Bentley Street. This was because the stop at the bottom of the hill was a fare stage, and if they had tried to ride to the top of the hill they would have had to pay an extra half penny.

This was not in any way meanness. It just emphasised the low incomes of the working people and the lengths they took to watch every penny.

George Morton

Mam

Life was not as easy in years gone by as it is now. It was precious and more precarious. Mam was born on 19 February 1914. Before she was six months old her father was killed whilst fishing; he was mate on the M/T *Dovey*. Adoption then was not an option as it is now. A large family who could not cope with a new addition would farm out that child to another family for them to bring up as their own. So it was with Mam. No adoption papers, no local authorities; just an informal agreement.

Throughout her childhood, Mam was sent every week to a house in Blundell Avenue to fetch four shillings which she understood was for her weekly allowance. She took the money back to her 'home' in Tiverton Street and handed it to her 'mum and dad'. At the age of about fourteen it occurred to her to ask the people who gave her the money why they should be contributing to her upkeep. They explained that they were her true parents and were paying towards her meals and upkeep. Her 'mum and dad' duly confirmed this. It was quite a shock. During the times when money was always short, relationships meant more. Her lifelong friend up to that stage was Mark, perhaps a year or two older than she was. Upon hearing the news that Mam was from the other house, he jumped for joy, telling everyone who would listen. You see, this lifelong good friend was actually her real brother. They had been together for fourteen years and had not known. This incident bonded the two together for the rest of their lives.

Mam went to Elliston Street Girls' School, and I still have her cookery exercise book dated 1929. A recipe for milk pudding includes an ingredient called 'cornflower mould', and the instruction that 'cauliflower must be cooked upside-down'. A recipe for Irish stew contains scrag-end of neck.

By the age of fourteen she was working as a housemaid for a retired army captain, who lived in a sort of mansion at Healing. Sunday was a day off from work. However, being an accomplished pianist, she had taken on the job of organist and pianist at the Lovett Street chapel where there was the Fisherman's Mission. With three services to attend each Sunday, the day was hard work. This was further exacerbated as her reputation grew and she was asked to stand in for absent pianists and organists at other churches as well. It meant running from one church to the next. It gave her no real day off from working, or for the chance to be at home.

When she died in 1993 I inherited the family Bible. It contained what looks like our family history going back to 1775. As the first entries describe people in their twenties, our family is traceable back to the 1750s. Mam inserted home-made bookmarks between the pages. These were the words to various hymns cut out of church magazines or newspapers. The reverse of these slips of paper is as interesting as the front. Some give just the briefest glimpse of Grimsby and Cleethorpes at around the turn of the century and in the early decades of the twentieth century. One is about a medical officer presenting his report to the Urban Sanitary Authority in 1888, on the state of the health of the Cleethorpes-with-Thrunscoe population. People died of diseases such as cholera then. Smallpox, chickenpox and zymotic diseases are also mentioned. Another sheet of paper gives the programme for the Children's Demonstration held for the Jubilee service for Queen Victoria's reign, held in the People's Park. Other bookmarks are small coloured cards, which contain New Year's greetings.

David Jagger

A surprise exhibit!

My family often visited my uncle who lived in Bursar Street. One day he took us to the garages behind his house. There was a small fire engine out on display, which was normally kept in one of the garages. As far as I can remember it was pulled by hand.

David Bradley

Attending churches

I attended St Peter's Anglican Church from the age of four, but transferred to Mill Road Methodist when I was seven, where I joined the Girls' Life Brigade. I was a Sunday School teacher until I was married there at twenty-one in 1947. Our three daughters were baptised there. The church was demolished and rebuilt as St Andrew's, opening in 1980.

Iris Morton

Using the toilet

In the 1940s I remember visiting family relatives who used to live on Tetney Road, Humberstone (spelt with an 'e' in those days). Their house was next to the original church vicarage, but separated by an orchard. The house had only two rooms downstairs and two upstairs, and the toilet was a short walk across a yard behind the house. Toilets for the other houses were in another building. Each toilet had a wooden door, and inside, a wooden bench with a hole in it. A bucket was placed underneath the bench. Because we

St Peter's Church, Cleethorpes, before the memorial was built.

Station Road. New Waltham.

Station Road, New Waltham, looking towards Toll Bar. On the left beyond the level crossing can be seen the Harvest Moon public house.

were in the country, there was no water supply to flush the waste away. Any water required was obtained from a pump in the shared backyard.

I don't remember if the bucket was emptied into the 'stink cart' or if the contents were used as fertiliser on the garden.

Whilst doing some research for my family history I was loaned a book entitled *Humberstone, The Story of a Village*, compiled by Arthur E. Kirkby, dated 1953. The house mentioned above was one of six almshouses that were built from a bequest of Matthew Humberstone. Among others to benefit was the Humberstone foundation school at Clee (Boys' Grammar School, Clee Road, Cleethorpes). Later, some money from Humberstone's charity funds was used to supplement money that had come from public funds to build the Cleethorpes Secondary School for Girls on Clee Road.

David Bradley

Village life

I lived in Peaks Lane, New Waltham, and went to Peaks Lane Primary School from the age of three. I passed my eleven–plus and went to Clee Grammar in 1950, where I stayed for two terms. I moved to Hymers College, Hull, at Easter 1951 and commuted to school weekly during the summer term by train and ferry. With Saturday morning school, I was home in New Waltham for less than thirty hours a week. We moved to Hull in the summer.

My father was a teacher at Grimsby Nautical College, and during the war he also taught at evening classes. He became Principal of Hull Nautical College at Easter 1951.

As well as additional evening teaching, my father did fire-watching two nights a week at the Nautical School during the war. I used to meet him coming back in the morning. I remember the air raids. At school we had concrete shelters in the playing field into which we went. At home we had a metal shelter which was also a dining table (a Morrison shelter). A bomb fell near the railway station and demolished at least one house.

Next door to our house in New Waltham was the village shop, Skelton's. I remember queuing there for hours. Just a little further along Peak's Lane lived Roger Smalley, with whom I still exchange Christmas greetings. Now the houses are numbered. The row of houses finished at a field across which I used to cycle to Grimsby. The footpath came out at the bottom of Hainton Avenue. For some years I cycled each Saturday for piano lessons, and then visited my maternal grandfather in Grimsby.

During the war a bomb dropped in the field next to Peak's Lane, across which I began my cycle ride. This caused a large crater. At the far end of the field was a farm where I went to collect straw for my pet rabbit. Further on, a mile from our house was a crossroads. This was the extremity of my tricycle rides as a younger child. On turning right I was in the countryside. The other extremity was Toll Bar School, again about a mile away. To reach there I had to cross the railway level crossing at New Waltham station. This was a special haunt for me when my Uncle Norman was a temporary stationmaster and when a school friend lived at the station house. I was a frequent visitor to the signal box.

Near to the station were a gentlemen's hairdresser (on the right going from our house, on the Humberston side) and a newsagent for the delivery of papers. There was a church on each side of Peaks Lane school. We attended the Methodist chapel when petrol rationing prevented our going to Hainton Avenue Church in Grimsby. I went three times on a Sunday, often with a prayer meeting following the evening service. My mother was a local preacher and pianist at the Women's meeting. My grandmother also attended the Women's

meeting. She lived at 'Penrhyn' off Station Avenue, which was then an unmade road.

Between our house and the school was Adams dairy, though we had our milk delivered by the Co-op! On the other side of the road was the 'wireless station' with masts 300 feet high. Families lived in the houses there. These children were fortunate to have their fathers with them, and not away at the war. They provided children's parties at Christmas and peace celebrations.

Revd Roy Allison

Romance blossomed

When we moved to Grimsby in 1960 I attended Flottergate Methodist Church, and there I met my future husband. I remember the first time he asked me for a date. We took a trolleybus from the old market place to Cleethorpes Bathing Pool. We sat on the top deck – something that I did not usually do. This added to the excitement. On reaching Cleethorpes we walked along the seafront and after a while went and sat on a seat in Ross Castle watching the sea. It was a lovely evening and one of those times I will always remember. This was the first of many visits to Cleethorpes during our courtship, which are both memorable and exciting.

Sandra Leonard

Scouting in Cleethorpes

Ron Driver has sent a copy of an article that appeared in *The News* dated Wednesday 13 January 1971. It documents the history of the Scouting movement in Cleethorpes, including the formation of the first Sea Scout troop in the world.

The movement began when three boys met in a shelter on the promenade in 1907. The group expanded, and at the beginning of the

St Aiden's Scout Camp at Riby Park in 1912.

First World War many lads tried to join the forces, but were too young. Instead eight enrolled in the Coastguards which allowed some of the men to join the Royal Navy.

In 1954 Fred Pinder of Sheffield, veteran of the 1908-1918 troop, met up with Fred Appleyard and organised the first reunion which attracted twenty-five former Scouts and some former leaders.

Ron Driver collects Scout and Guide memorabilia and is a recognised authority on the history of these organisations.

Stories from mother

My mother, Ada Robinson, left St John's School in 1900 at the age of twelve. The family lived at the bottom end of Suggitt's Lane, which in those days was a mud lane. Grandfather Robinson used to carry mother and her two sisters, Adelaide and Ruth, up the lane – especially if it was wet and muddy – to Grimsby Road. The three girls then walked to school, which for them was St John's School in Grimsby.

They had some friends called Brown who lived in a house over Suggitt's Lane crossing on the sands. When there was a high tide, the sea water came into the Brown family's kitchen, but they had a pump which went down so deep in the ground that their drinking water was not affected.

Every so often a soldier would come down the lane and tell the householders to open all their windows, as the army would be doing some target practice on the beach. The targets would be placed at the water's edge, then the cannon would come charging down and commence firing.

Granddad Robinson worked at one of the brick pits. There were two – Chapman's and Goods. Some sort of dispute occurred and they became Chapman's. Mam said the men working at the bottom of the pit looked like little ants crawling about. They struck a spring in the bottom but could not stop the flow of water, so gradually the pit filled up. At one time there were two waggoners' cottages over on the far side of the pit but they became submerged. Mother always said the brick pit was as deep as Cleethorpes' water tower was high.

One of the main highlights when she was young was going with Granddad to Flottergate Methodist Church in Grimsby to hear a special preacher – I think it was Tom Holland. They walked all the way there and back.

Joyce Tyson

Renaming Peter

The Revd Dr Frank Baker, who wrote a book on the history of Cleethorpes and became the world's leading expert on John Wesley, was minister of Trinity Methodist Church in St Peter's Avenue. His wife Nellie was my mother's cousin so I sometimes went to their home in Queen's Parade.

They had a dog called Peter but when Auntie Nellie gave birth to a son they called him Peter, too. The dog's name had to be changed – to Scamp. His most annoying habit was to run round in circles chasing his tail.

John D. Beasley

Revd Frank Baker is seen outside Trinity Methodist Church on St Peter's Avenue, Cleethorpes. His motorised bicycle was ideal for visiting the large circuit of churches in an area that was relatively flat. One of the preachers for Sunday 17 June is Geoffrey Joycey, who now lives in Winnipeg, Canada. Frank Baker's daughter, Enid Hickingbotham, thinks the year was 1952. She recalls that Frank flew in a small plane over Cleethorpes to take aerial photographs for his book.

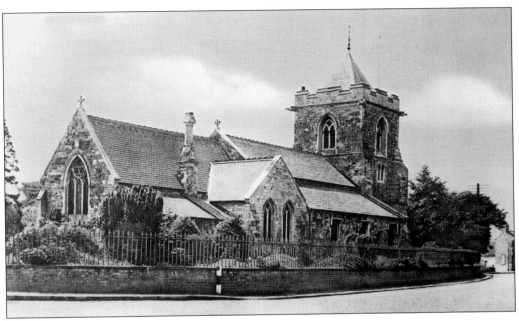

All Saints Church, Waltham, before the railings were removed. The postcard was sent by Jenny to Craig Joyce of Corby in February 1972, and franked with the slogan 'Happy family holidays'.

Tired of waiting

My earliest recollection was when I was four or five years old. After lunch my mum always did the washing up. On this particular day she seemed to be talking for ages. I got fed up with waiting and as I felt tired I got the tea cosy as a pillow and covered myself with the table-cloth. When my mum came out of the kitchen there I was fast asleep lying on the peg rug. To this day I can remember doing this and we often had a laugh over it.

Mary Barker

Tin baths

We take bathrooms, hot water and inside toilets for granted these days. When I was a kid living in Lovett Street, all we had was a tin bath that we put in front of the fire in the kitchen. There was no privacy for us kids getting washed or dried, with brothers and sisters waiting for their turn. Mam used to top up the water with some more hot, but we used the same water really. It was a bit tough on kids in large families – my pal Eileen was one of seven and the boys bathed one night and the girls the next.

The problem was heating enough water. Before we had a gas boiler (called a 'copper'), Mam heated water in a brick boiler in the scullery. It had to be stoked with coke or coal, and the water took hours to get hot. Then Mam had to lift the water out with a bucket. There was no tap. She used the same boiler for washing our clothes.

Mam used to tell us that during the war, they were allowed only a few inches of water in their tin bath. It soon went cold and they couldn't soak in it.

The bath was always stored on a hook on the wall in the back yard. Mam had to rinse it out before we used it. I never heard of a bath being stolen, even when people didn't have one of their own. People were much more honest and thoughtful in those days.

Sally Russell

Garden ornament dropped

When my lovely niece was very young, she dropped a stone dog on my head while I was lying on my mother's lawn in her Parker Street garden. I yelled with the shock but lived to tell the tale. My niece had no idea that she nearly killed her Uncle John, but we laugh about the incident whenever I remind her of it now.

John D. Beasley

Living through the twentieth century

Born in Cleethorpes in 1900, Charles Light was an only child, but part of a close-knit community of extended family, neighbours and school friends. He attended the Bursar Street school, which had opened in 1902. At its centenary, Charles sent a letter of greeting; and he was by far the oldest 'old boy'. His boyhood was happy and uneventful. He left school at fourteen to join the building firm Wilkinson and Houghton and trained as a joiner and carpenter.

During the early part of the First World War, Charles was a St John's messenger. He cycled furiously to the Grimsby headquarters with the news of the bombing of the Baptist church in 1916. He could recall sitting in a shelter on Cleethorpes' seafront watching a Zeppelin pass overhead. In 1918 he was called up to serve in the Sherwood Foresters.

For many years Cleethorpes was greatly influenced if not dominated by the Methodists – Prims and Wesleyans. It was natural to find friends in the church, which was the centre of social life.

After the First World War, Charles was one of the young set in the Wesleyan Methodist Church in St Peter's Avenue. They were halcyon days. There was a deep commitment to the service of the church in the Boy's Brigade, Sunday School and the Wesley Guild, matched by a similar zest for cycling, tennis, dancing on the pier, motor cycling and grass-track racing.

In 1922 Charles and Margaret were married and lived in Park View, Cleethorpes. Charles

St Aiden's Church, Grimsby Road, as seen from the Ritz Cinema, opposite.

Sidney Park was named after Sidney College, Cambridge which owned much of the local land. Children and adults have always enjoyed its ornamental lake.

obtained a grant to build his own house, Charnwood, on Laceby Road, Grimsby, next door to The Firs. These were the first houses beyond Tate's store at Nun's Corner. The materials cost £400. They moved there in 1926. By marrying Margaret, Charles acquired a new set of brothers, sister, aunts, cousins and spouses.

The depression of the thirties was a difficult period, though there was quite a lot of building in the town, in Nunsthorpe and around Bradley Cross Roads. It was at this time that Charles and Margaret decided to join the new Methodist Church at Bradley Cross Road. Charles made the pulpit, table and lectern for the new church.

Then came the Second World War. Charles took on what was to be a paramedic role at the first aid post in Nunsthorpe. He camouflaged his car in olive green, and it preserved the bodywork.

A bigger change took place in 1942. Charles was recruited by the Air Ministry to supervise the construction and maintenance of airfields in Lincolnshire. The work demanded gifts of management and leadership to get the job done. Typically, these skills were exercised with modesty and without fuss.

There were changes on the home front too. Charnwood became a popular home-from-home for Polish, Canadian and American aircrew. From these simple acts of kindness have sprung lifelong friendships.

Charles finally retired in 1960, though he oversaw the building of the Laceby bypass shortly after. He and Margaret hooked up their van and toured Britain. This was no new passion as in 1941 he had designed and built a trailer tent (very similar to a 1990 model).

In 1992 Charles decided to give up touring – he was worried that the van might be getting past it. This was also the year of their platinum wedding anniversary – seventy marvellous years. The family albums are full of great celebrations – golden, diamond, sixty-fifth and then the big seventy – all shared with friends and relations, and with frequent visits from mayoral parties.

Margaret's death in 1996 closed that chapter. Charles gave up his car and bought an electric buggy. He used it to visit the local library, Morrison's and church. He cooked, cleaned and soldiered on 'til 1999, when he decided to move.

Charles Light died in October 2002, aged 102. His life centred on his extended family and his deep commitment to the work of Christ at Laceby Road Methodist Church. The love of the people and shared concern meant so much to him, particularly during the years he was alone.

Tony Light

2 Streets and Businesses

Animal lovers save foxes

A turkey farmer at Donna Nook decided he must go to Cleethorpes one afternoon to collect some dry cleaning. It was late October and his birds were fattening up nicely for the Christmas market. The weather was warm for the time of year, so he left the barn door open and put a metre-high wire netting 'door' against the opening to allow plenty of ventilation.

On his way down the road towards Marshchapel, he passed a furniture lorry from Nottingham. He wondered who was moving into the area and which house they had bought.

After collecting his dry cleaning, he made his way back to his farm. The sight that met him made him physically sick. Of the hundred or so turkeys he had in the barn, only a handful remained alive. The rest were dead or dying – many were mutilated. His year's work was

This is one of seven postcards of 'Union Day at Grimsby', and shows the Cleethorpes' corner of Brereton Avenue opposite, with Park Street running left to right. It was taken from Oxford Street, Grimsby, and the site across the road in front of the photographer has been a petrol filling station for many years.

St Peter's Avenue. The houses on the left were later converted to shops. Number 7 would be in this first block.

gone. It was too late to restock for Christmas. How had this happened?

Eventually the truth came out. Animal lovers around Nottingham had wanted to clear the area of an over-abundance of foxes. They had humanely trapped over five dozen, but could not kill them; that's cruel. Someone had a wonderful idea: 'Let's release them into the countryside where they can live as nature intended.'

They hired a furniture van, put the foxes in the back then drove to a place where the foxes could roam free – Donna Nook in the wilds of Lincolnshire. There the foxes were released and ran off across the fields.

Your imagination will tell you what happened next. Some of the foxes picked up the scent of the turkeys on the wind and searched them out. In less than fifteen minutes, the instinct of the foxes took over and they chased, bit and slaughtered almost all the turkeys – for sport. None of the turkeys was eaten.

The farmer's livelihood had been destroyed. It was too late in the season to start again. Birds of the age and weight that he needed would be too expensive to buy. His business was finished.

This act was carried out by animal lovers, who, on their way back to Nottingham would be congratulating themselves on solving the problem of the poor foxes.

Simon Drake

Telephones in New Waltham

I remember the time when telephones were few. I believe my parents ordered one before the war, but it had not been installed by the time we moved in 1951. I think the shop had one, and so did the doctor who lived not far away. The only other phone I remember was in the public box near the post office on Peaks

Lane, near the junction with Station Road. We used this one.

Revd Roy Allison

A wonderful business

My aunt had a milliner's shop at No. 7 St Peter's Avenue, which is now Comley's Cameras. I used to live above the shop with my parents when I was a small boy. She retired from the business in 1953 and leased the shop to Willey's Pet Stores until they retired from business. The property was sold to Healey and Bakers, Property Developers, for £30,000 which was considered a small fortune in those days. Aunt's husband had a private mobile lending library called The Beacon Lending Library in the 1930s.

Miss Everett's was a wonderful business. People used to come to Cleethorpes for the day by train, call in at my aunt's shop for a fitting, and hopefully the hat would be made before they left for home at teatime. If the hat could not be completed in time, my uncle would take it to the parcels' office for onward despatch by passenger train.

Among other keepsakes, I still have the gate that went across the doorway at night, and the stamps used on the mobile library.

Incidentally, my aunt's shop was the very first down St Peter's Avenue that was not situated on the corner of a street, being the first mid-terrace house to be converted to a shop in the 1920s.

Jim Everett

Jim and his wife Pam are members of the Cleethorpes Catering Cuties, an 'august body of former seaside landladies and men' who used to put on shows at the Pier Pavilion when it was used as a theatre. Each

Doug Comley (left) outside his shop on the corner of Kingsway and Brighton Street, with visitors from Belgium.

year the *Cuties* also did a summer season at the Winter Gardens with Jack Lawton and Shirley King.

The *Cuties* were the brainchild of Les Robinson, who, with his wife Jessy, ran the Haffenden Guest House on the Kingsway at the corner of Bradford Avenue.

Ignorance led to a fine

The only time I have been fined was for an offence I committed in Cleethorpes – without realising I was breaking the law.

My dear Mum moved from Scartho to Cleethorpes and loved living in Parker Street. On one occasion when I was staying with her, I parked my car outside her bungalow and later was upset to find a fixed penalty notice on it. Without realising that it was an offence, I had parked my car facing the wrong way overnight. I was fined £6 when that was quite a lot of money.

My mother felt pleased and much safer in the knowledge that the police patrolled her street at night.

John D. Beasley

Braiding nets

My aunt, Violet Pougher, was born in 1905. During 1940 she worked in a munitions factory. The explosives that she had to handle stained her hands yellow. After the war she followed in her mother's footsteps and worked for the Great Grimsby Coal Salt and Tanning Company, braiding trawler nets.

She lived at No. 40 Eleanor Street, Grimsby, where she had a braiding pole installed in the kitchen. A lorry came once a week to collect the finished work, and delivered raw materials for the coming week. Before becoming a skilled braider, girls were employed as 'fillers'. Their job was to fill the needles ready for the

braider to use. After watching and learning the skills and methods, they became braiders themselves. On one occasion, the girls made a specially-designed animal net for use in Rhodesia.

Roy Shaw

Our changing road system

I talked myself into this one. I was discussing road developments in north-east Lincolnshire with Brian Leonard, and complaining about recently introduced deliberate bottlenecks. 'Write it down for the book,' he said… I looked at the picture of the old road junction to Tetney in Humberston. Though visits to Grimsby or Louth would have been rare in those days, carts and early motors would have negotiated such corners with ease. However, I can imagine some people having a shock as an early Morris suddenly appeared round the blind corner and confronted a timid pony (not to say its owner!). The wide junction now allows drivers to see clearly and traffic to flow freely on all routes.

Alan Fisher

Poor planning

In New Waltham the forty miles-per-hour speed limit has been reduced to thirty miles-per-hour, a good idea. But to then reduce the capacity of the bypass to one slow lane has simply caused traffic to continue using the route through the village. Motorists coming from the Hewitt's Circus direction do not want to sit in a long queue leading up to the Toll Bar bottleneck. This is a typical example of poor planning.

Alan Fisher

Violet Pougher and nephew Roy Shaw walking along Station Approach in Cleethorpes, around 1948.

Passing trade

In Waltham, the main road dips through the village centre and needs the pelican crossing to allow pedestrians to cross safely. Here we see another side to the 'all villages must have a bypass' argument. With traffic having to go through this village, local shops benefit. I remember returning from days out with the family in the 1970s and regularly stopping off at the old Frying Pan fish and chip shop in the High Street. I'm sure Waltham shopkeepers would readily admit that they do benefit from the passing trade. More trade means shops stay open.

Alan Fisher

Quiet village life

The Laceby bypass made a lot of difference to traffic using the A46 and to Laceby village. It reduced journey times for through traffic, reduced the wear and tear on the vehicles and caused less pollution. The benefit to Laceby village was immense. Having buses and heavy lorries negotiating its narrow roads and tight, awkward corners was a nightmare for residents and travellers alike. When the traffic used the 'new' road, village life returned to its pre-war atmosphere and gentle tranquillity. Life was safer for all concerned.

Further along the A46, Irby-upon-Humber, Swallow and Caistor benefited in the same way.

Great Coates' new bypass cut the community in two, but was a sensible shortcut. It separated St Nicolas' Church and some houses on Aylesby Road from the rest of the village, but thanks to enthusiastic clergy the church is still very much part of the village 'across the road'.

At Stallingborough, the new road was again taken away from the village, and a big round-about put in to allow traffic to and from the Humber factories to cross Healing-Immingham traffic easily. Even at busy times the flow round the island is rarely held up. Current policy might have dictated traffic lights instead! All Healing-Immingham traffic misses the village, though heavy traffic still goes through the village on its way to the Humber bank factories.

Traffic passing Healing has never disturbed the residential area. The village developed between the road and the railway station. It is still a quiet village off the beaten track, though the main road is close by. New estates have been developed alongside the old.

Louth Road twists and turns through Holton-le-Clay and was a constant cause of congestion. Here is another example of common sense taking the through traffic away from the houses and shops, and making the village quieter and safer. Drivers do not suffer the frustration and danger of crawling along narrow, congested streets.

Alan Fisher

Having alternatives

A good road infrastructure is essential to life in the twenty-first century, despite what our

The corner of Humberstone Avenue and Tetney Road (left) before any widening took place. On the right is the Methodist chapel built on 'The Little Clover', land which was given by Lord Carrington in 1907. The building of red brick and blue slate with Gothic windows is still in use. Previously services were held in a chapel in Wendover Lane, the land also having been given by Lord Carrington, lord of the manor. That chapel was opened on 25 July 1835 by James Henwood of Hull and Revd James Methley. A small schoolroom was added on the north side in 1896. The building is now known as Wendover Hall.

In 1938 a Morris Eight collided with this water fountain, causing it to be demolished. Built before 1910, it had previously stood at the top of Sea Road.

council tells us. Years ago, our grandparents did not travel as far as we expect to today. Communities were more compact, and, because personal transport had not developed, people could rely on a good public transport system. If we are to be persuaded to leave our cars at home, there has to be a comprehensive and sensible bus and train alternative. Until then, we must use our cars.

Alan Fisher

Many uses

From 1870 the pier was the main venue for entertainment and its offerings became more diverse. The Empire on Alexandra Road opened as the Alexandra Hall Theatre in 1896.

A local group opened the Coliseum in the High Street to show films, but from the time of the First World War, it too diversified and was used for boxing matches of the Manchester Regiment which was billeted in Cleethorpes during the war. In 1919 the Cleethorpes Empire Co. Ltd bought the building, restoring film shows. When the company acquired the Theatre Royal in 1926 the Coliseum became the British Legion club, and continued to serve various functions until 1952 when it became a store.

From research by David Bradley

Stopped by village bobby

After travelling around the East Riding of Yorkshire in 1969 with a friend, Peter Thewlis, we caught the ferry from Hull to New Holland Pier. We then had a wet ride along country roads in north-east Lincolnshire. As we cycled through Healing, the 'village bobby' suddenly stepped out from behind a signpost and called: 'Where are you going?'

Puzzled, but not wanting to cause problems, we answered, 'Home'. The bobby relaxed and, after a friendly chat, we were allowed to continue cycling on to our homes in Grimsby.

At home, my Mum was relieved nothing worse had happened.

John D. Beasley

The Appleyard family

Amos Appleyard moved to Cleethorpes and became a local Methodist preacher. His gravestone can still be seen in Old Clee churchyard. For a while he ran the Yarra Road post office, before taking over the wet fish shop in Cambridge Street.

He became involved in the annual Cleethorpes Carnival Parade in the 1920s, taking great pleasure in decorating his shop especially for the occasion. The shops were judged during the parade.

Fred Appleyard's wet fish shop in Cambridge Street, decorated to celebrate the Silver Jubilee of King George V and Queen Mary in 1935. The display was all Fred's own work.

Fred Appleyard all prepared for his ride in a 1930s Cleethorpes Carnival Parade.

His son, Fred, my father, took over the business and continued the tradition.

During the war I remember having to go to Grimsby fish docks to get fish for Dad to sell in the shop. I used to have to go by bus and carry it, two stone at a time, in a wicker basket.

Fred Appleyard's shop was where the car park is on Cambridge Street, with Gott's butchers next door. Then there was an alleyway (an 'eight foot') with Boyes on the other side. That was owned by a man with red eyes. Penistone's was on the corner of Seaview Street with the Meadow on the opposite corner. Other premises I remember include Councillor Cox's grocery shop, the Salvation Army, a florist, and on the corner of Wardle Street was an ironmonger's. You were a 'Meggie' if you were born between the top of High Cliff and the Boating Lake on the seaward side of Oxford Street.

Vera Thorpe

Exploring by bike

When I was a teenager (in the sixties), I biked all over Cleethorpes, mainly following the bus routes. I never thought to buy a street map, but I enjoyed riding along unfamiliar streets, seeing different shops and houses. I especially liked exploring the new estates and often wondered if I would ever live on one.

I sometimes think I would like to ride around those same estates nowadays. But today there are gangs of youths hanging about who are only too keen to threaten older people. In groups they are brave and strong. I heard of one elderly man who was pushed off his bike so the youths could steal it. The world is a different place now, and not for the better.

Mr E. Smith

Working on The Fitties

Before 1962, to me Cleethorpes was just the town next to Grimsby. It had a fine sandy beach and ended at the Bathing Pool, or so I thought.

In the spring of 1962 I became a weekend caravan salesman. This was my first introduction to The Fitties, and it was to change my life. Until then, I had thought of a caravan as a box on wheels that people towed behind a car.

After two years I became the manager. My full-time employment started on 8 February 1964, during an appalling winter. I began to wonder if I had made the right choice. I was not used to working on my own in the middle of nowhere. Some days I would not see another living soul.

The camps did not open until 15 March. Caravan owners began to drift back and life was returning. The weather also began to get better, and some days even the sun would shine.

The holiday homes were very primitive – no utilities and they had only an earth toilet in a shed at the bottom of the garden. Though some people had a small television, it ran off a car battery. It was like a step back in time.

There were compensations, however. There were no shops, no amusements nor any other commercial distractions. It was just peace, perfect peace.

One of my favourite memories is of walking around The Fitties camp on a Sunday morning. There was the sound of happy children playing and the delicious smell of breakfast cooking. The smell of bacon and eggs made me forget that I had had my own breakfast already.

Compared to today, it was very austere. Living there was an escape for a lot of working-class people. I think the majority of people were miners. They used to tell me that one of the reasons they came was for the fresh air.

A postcard of Alexandra Road which was postmarked on 9 May 1905 in Gillingham, Kent.

Their working environment was very polluted.

I must admit that I took life there for granted. People wore any old clothes, and pastimes were very simple: fishing in the creek, building sandcastles, cockling or just paddling in the sea. Halcyon times of just loafing about! The habit of visiting the seaside was passed down from generation to generation.

Come Saturday night it was a change of scene. After a good scrub-up, it was on with the best suit and a walk down to the Beacholme or Seymour's club. If they were not drinkers, they would probably have a stroll along the promenade.

One of my earliest memories is of my first customer. It was a very quiet day so I put the kettle on to make a cup of tea. A young man came into the yard and said he was interested in buying a well-known make of touring car-

avan. I completed the sale. I remember he was a local civil servant. I can even recall his name. After he had left, I remembered that I had been making a cup of tea. I rushed into the caravan office to find that the bottom of the kettle had burnt away. I suppose the good thing was that the caravan had not burnt down!

One of my initial difficulties was in understanding the south-west Yorkshire accent. Some were broader than others but I soon got used to it. I quickly learnt that the miners called a spade a spade. I was not used to people being so blunt. I soon found out that if I talked to them the same way they talked, I got on fine. I would like to think that a lot of them became friends as well as customers.

Some customers were a bit unusual. After paying for a caravan, one asked for some luck money. That was a new one on me. He expected me to give him a pound or two back.

35

A Daimler single-deck bus travels through The Fitties camp, c.1960. Note the wooden chalets with brick chimney stacks, glass verandas and simple fencing.

I explained that I could not do that as I had already made out the receipt.

In the early days, the only form of heating was a coal fire. This was fine for the miners who were given an allowance of free coal, and would bring a bag every time they came. Whenever I visited their caravans, whether in winter or summer, the fire would be blazing away. It was their way of life. They could not understand why I complained of the heat.

The summers seemed endless. Eventually, towards the end of the season when the dark nights drew in, the camp would become transformed. In the dark it was like fairyland. There were no street lights, but from each caravan came shafts of light. In the glare of car headlights I would see literally hundreds of rabbits.

The working days in the summer were extremely long. A twelve-hour day was normal. This meant I saw very little of my children. By the time I arrived home, they were tucked up in bed. After a long, tiring hot summer I looked forward to the winter, knowing that my working hours would be shorter. However, halfway through the winter I would be wishing for the spring to come.

I spent thirty-two years working on The Fitties, and left only when I retired. I saw many changes. When I started, caravans were just small boxes on wheels. Now they are up to forty-five feet long. They have all modern services: water, electricity, toilets, cookers, fridges, showers and gas fires. What a transformation in thirty-two years! What will they be like after the next thirty-two?

Ah well, happy days!

David Edwards

3 Visiting

Always made welcome

I visited Cleethorpes on holiday with my parents and brother during the late forties and early fifties and I have very happy memories of those times.

We stayed full board, as I think most holidaymakers did in those days, with Bert and Betty Henley on Mill Road. Somewhere in the archives, I have photos of them and also of their two daughters, Joan and Marlene. Joan, the elder girl, was studying to be a doctor I believe. I remember her as a tall, statuesque young lady with golden-red hair. Marlene was tall and slim with dark hair, and remains in my memory as being comparable to the character Jo in *Little Women*.

Holidays were very simple in those days. After breakfast we went out to the beach where we made sandcastles and played cricket. I have a photo of myself somewhere on a poor horse called Whisky – I was rather a chubby child!

We took trips down to Wonderland, where my favourite stall was 'Bunty pulls a string'. Just behind the counter was a 'horse's tail' collection of the ends of strings. The strings stretched overhead to the back of the stall. The idea was to pull a string and hope that your string was attached to a prize. I usually won a prize, albeit not a very expensive one.

I remember the Henleys as hard-working, caring people. They always made us welcome, and we loved our few holidays there.

One of our holidays with them was tinged with sadness. They had a lovely Alsatian dog which was knocked down, and I believe killed, whilst we were there.

One other poignant memory is of us walking home on summer's evenings along the length of Kingsway. There were lavender bushes on one side and my mother always pressed a flower between her fingers to smell the gentle perfume. Lavender still brings back that vivid memory.

On a funnier note, my grandma came and stayed over one night whilst we were on holiday. The Henleys were fully booked up, so grandma stayed a little way up the road. I still remember her horror as she told us that when her landlady gave her fish for tea, the parsley sauce was made with water instead of milk!

As I said, holidays then were gentler and less frenetic than ones taken today. There was a limited amount of money to be spent on deckchairs, ice creams, slot machines and sending postcards home. Overall, without looking through rose-coloured glasses, I remember our summer holidays in Cleethorpes with much affection and with many happy memories.

I hope my small contribution is of interest. It has made me feel good remembering.

Anne Reynolds

A very crowded beach. Note how many of these visitors wore hats and formal dress.

Always lots to do

In the summer holidays my friend and I always go to Cleethorpes because her mum owns a rock shop and her dad owns a chip shop. We go to work with her mum and play on the beach while she is serving. It's really fun because there are lots of things for us to do.

One time we bought some chips from the chippie and had a picnic on the beach. We went to the bouncy castle and because it was so hot we splashed in the water to cool off.

We never get bored in the holidays because there's always something to do at Cleethorpes.

Leigh French
(aged ten)

My second home

I have lots of happy memories of my childhood in Cleethorpes, as I spent every holiday there for years. I first went when I was about two years old; my brother who is ten years older first went when he was five years old. We used to stay in a boarding house in Thrunscoe Road. It was like going home.

There were always tears at the end of the holiday as I never wanted to come home. My first recollection is of catching a steam train at Sheffield Victoria station. They always seemed to be packed with people and sometimes we had to stand in the corridor until we could get a seat.

On arrival at Cleethorpes we would find a 'barrow boy' who could take our luggage on a handcart to 'our house'. The first thing we did was to go shopping for our food, at the Maypole and Meadow Dairies on Cambridge Street. We used to go to a dairy nearby for the milk.

One year when we arrived by train there was a problem with the case barrow. We had found a barrow boy as usual and put our cases on the barrow, but as we went along one of the wheels started to wobble. It gradually got worse and just before we arrived at the house, the wheel came off. The poor lad was in such a state, apologetic and near to tears. My dad joked with him and paid him a good tip to make up for it.

There were no mod cons in the early years. At bedtime we used to have a nightlight candle on a saucer on the washstand. For washing we had a bowl and a jug of cold water. The toilet was down the yard outside. There was no electricity at that time just after the Second World War; gas mantles were lit to give light. Cooking was done on the Yorkshire range.

Tuesday afternoons were spent at Grimsby market and the shops in Freeman Street. The highlight of the week was going to Grimsby Docks and boarding the paddle steamer for a trip to Spurn Point and the Bull Fort.

We used to walk along Hardy's Lane (now Hardy's Road), the continuation of Thrunscoe Road to the farm, then through the fields to Humberston. Incidentally, my father stayed in the Cowman's Cottage at the same farm for a while during the war. We walked back along the seafront past the meridian line and the Boating Lake in time for tea.

The early evenings were spent in Wonderland. I used to have six three penny bits to spend each night. What you could do with that amount in those days! There were slot machines, rides and games. I remember that there used to be a roller-skating rink and motorboats under the Big Dipper.

Near to Ross Castle, where the waterfall is now, was the Grotto Aquarium. The admission charge for a child was 3d.

No week was complete without a visit to see a good show at the Empire Theatre in Alexandra Road and to the Royal Cinema at the top of Station Approach.

I remember the old Bathing Pool and Café Dansant – now both gone; the paddling pool and sand pit, which I am pleased to see are still there; the cast-iron fountain opposite Brighton Street slipway, and the trolleybuses. Looking back, I don't know how we managed to fit everything into just a week. I also had time to play on the sands and go for a paddle. There was no time to be bored in those days. Although I do not go to Cleethorpes for holidays now, I still like to visit for a day's outing. I have seen a few changes over the last fifty-seven years, but it is still my second home.

Mary Barker

Pictures in the mind

I remember being excited when we went to Cleethorpes by train. The thrill really began after leaving Grimsby and then at Cleethorpes we saw the sea so near to the lines. There used to be lots of little shops all along the seafront selling sticks of rock, gifts, shellfish, newspapers and comics.

I can still picture the rows of fishing boats in the Humber morning and evening, passing the forts that protected the river mouth.

Mrs B. Morley

A mixture of visitors

I ran a guesthouse for almost seventeen years and I enjoyed it most of the time. We had four available rooms; one was just a double-bedded room, but the other three could accommodate two adults and up to three children. On the ground floor there was a sitting room, dining room and the kitchen. My husband and I lived in the attic during the holiday season. It didn't seem as cramped as you would think, but I suppose we got used to it.

The families who came varied tremendously. Some were so quiet that we hardly knew they were there. They came in, spoke quietly through their meals, and made no sound at all when they were in their rooms. Others were just the opposite. One Doncaster family I can still remember vividly today. All of their conversations were conducted by shouting at each other. The wife often used to tell her husband that he was deaf, and that always annoyed him. He clearly had a hearing problem, but would not admit it. He usually replied 'Yerwat?' to whatever you said to him. The two boys were polite enough, but conducted all their conversations so everyone else heard every word. It was very interesting to hear them talk about their Dad: we could hear what they were saying but he was totally oblivious! We all breathed a sigh of relief when they went out for the day, and we dreaded the time when they returned.

Occasionally a couple would arrive and act very sheepishly. Within an hour we had usually worked out whether they were just timid, newly married, or having a naughty week away. These last sorts always booked in as 'Mr and Mrs' in those days (the fifties), and despite having all the outwards signs of being married, there was always something that gave them away. Sometimes we picked up casual remarks like, 'When you get back to your house, tell your mother...' or 'Do you have one sugar or two?' Other couples were very noisy in bed, and sometimes blushed constantly at breakfast. They were not always young people either. Many of those having an affair were in their late twenties or thirties. We would sometimes overhear remarks about a partner, such as

Despite the dull day, plenty of people are making the most of the Bathing Pool.

'He/She isn't like he/she used to be' or 'I wish I had married you instead.' However, all was not always lovey-dovey with such pairs. One couple had an argument halfway through the week, admitted all, and left spitting abuse at each other!

People would tell us what they had been doing all day. As long as it was fine, most were content to sit on the sand and enjoy the sunshine and the view. Some said how much they enjoyed the sea breeze which was much more refreshing than the city air of the Midlands. Some would want to know where the town's parks and gardens were, and enjoy their time playing games on the grass. Others would go on a mystery coach tour, and come back with tales of the villages and sights they had seen. Those who came regularly got to know the area, and would go to Grimsby or Louth on market day. They didn't necessarily buy much, but seemed to enjoy wandering round the shops and stalls.

Wet days were more of a problem, and east-coast summers can have whole weeks of rain. The kids loved to go to Wonderland, to ride on the dodgems, play on the slot machines and so on. This was not so much fun for their parents, especially day after day. Some used to be concerned about the expense. I felt so sorry for those who had had a miserable day and came back wet through and fed up. It wasn't possible to say, 'You can stay here and watch the television.' In the fifties there was only BBC, and telly programmes were very limited then.

During those years, I learnt a lot about how to handle people who had come away to stay in someone else's home. Despite all those who clearly had come to 'use' us, there were many who were respectful and appreciative. Some even came year after year, and it was always a pleasure to see them again.

Mrs P. Warren

Memorable tomato sandwiches

One of my strongest memories of Cleethorpes is of sitting on the beach eating home-made tomato sandwiches. I have eaten thousands of tomato sandwiches since then (as that was fifty years ago), but they never taste the same. I think what's missing is the tang of salt in the air, and the crunch of sand in the slices of bread!

Maureen Thompson

Skating on thin ice!

I remember the Boating Lake being frozen one winter. Three of us had trekked across town to see the area covered in snow and ice. We watched some other kids walking on the frozen lake. There was a cracking sound as one lad went nearer to the centre. He obviously heard it, because he paused and looked down at the ice he was standing on. Then, very cautiously, he turned back towards the shore. He was lucky the ice held his weight and he reached land safely. He said he knew the ice would hold him, but we knew he'd really been scared of falling through.

Carol Hurst

Arriving by train

I recall walking down to the railway station to watch the 'trip trains' arrive. On the right-hand side were the large houses of Victoria Terrace, which were demolished after the war. There seemed to be a train arriving every few minutes, each full of day trippers and weekly visitors. It was fun to see them pour out of the station and descend the steps to the beach, then fan out to find a space on the sands.

The men were usually dressed in their 'Sunday suits' wearing bowlers or flat caps, and occasionally trilbies. Their only concession to

The essence of Cleethorpes' attraction – a family group enjoying the sand.

the environment was to remove their shoes and socks and replace their hats with a cotton handkerchief. They rolled up their trouser legs for a paddle in the sea.

On the station forecourt young lads waited with home-made barrows on which the cases of the weekly visitors would be carried to the 'digs' for a few pence. Holidays were restricted to a week that had to be taken in the month of August. A week's unpaid holiday was all a man was entitled to in the thirties. Each town in the Midlands had a different week allocated to them. Thereby there was Sheffield Week, Doncaster Week, Barnsley Week and so on.

Iris Morton

The sun was always shining

I remember the Submarine public house, and the shops either side of the entrance to the Pier Pavilion, being built, I think, by Wilkinson and Houghton builders. My late father was a bricklayer on both sites, his nickname being 'Questie'. As a child I remember my mother taking my young brother and me to meet him during his lunch break and then eating ice cream while we walked along the promenade. The year was probably 1938 and in those days the sun was always shining!

Beryl Lusby (née Ainsworth)

A white dress is perfect for a hot day, though other people look better-protected from any cold winds. Iris Morton and her cousin Cissy walking along the prom in 1936.

I enjoyed it – really!

When I went to Pleasure Island with my friend it was really fun. We went on a swan boat – that was really funny. My friend and I got stuck because we crashed into the edge where it was muddy. Thankfully a man helped us. I had to grab his walking stick. It was so embarrassing. He was pulling and pulling but in the end it was all right.

Also I went on the Boomerang, a roller coaster. I wasn't very keen on going on it, but I did. It was awful. I just closed my eyes. I felt so sick.

Tiggy Trigg
(aged ten)

Holidays before the war

I remember when the Holiday with Pay Act came in. We could now afford to have a holiday too. We'd had days out before, but usually lost pay if we'd wanted some time off work. Our first proper week's holiday was spent staying in a guest house near my sister in Doncaster. We went by bus, and the journey took over three hours. There were some nice villages and towns on the way, and some long boring roads. There was a dreadful bottleneck the other side of Scunthorpe where the road narrowed and went under a railway bridge.

We'd chosen to stay with Mrs Cook, because she said she was only ten minutes from the bus station, but it was more than twenty with those cases, and Bill, our eleven-year-old son trailing along.

No one we knew ever went abroad in those days. The people at No. 22 went to Brighton the same year, just before the start of the war. They went by train and had to go across London on the underground. That journey took them nearly all day, and then they had a bus ride to their boarding house. They said they had enjoyed themselves. It had been much warmer on the south coast than up here in Lincolnshire. They had even gone to London for a day and seen the Houses of Parliament and Buckingham Palace but not the King or the princesses. That holiday had cost them a lot more than our holiday. We got better value.

My friend lived in Daubney Street, and they went to the Butlin's Holiday Camp. They didn't say much about the food, but they enjoyed all the fun. Their girl Jean won one of the competitions.

Dorothy Caufield

Condiments were extra

Cleethorpes' houses were mostly rented and the tenants would accommodate the visitors in their own bedrooms, often sleeping downstairs themselves or farming their children out to relatives in order to let their bedrooms also. Sometimes food was bought out, or brought in to be cooked by the landlady, and condiments were extra! The visitors were not welcome back in between meal times even when it was raining, as they would be in the way in a small house. The money made from the holiday visitors was to supplement the meagre wages people received in those days.

The large houses, such as those in Victoria Terrace, catered for the 'better class' of visitors.

Iris Morton

Cleethorpes railway station with its clock tower, and Victoria Terrace beyond.

Much to enjoy

'We are going on holiday to Cleethorpes', my father would announce, and immediately our spirits rose. We really looked forward to this holiday because all our uncles, aunts and cousins lived in Lincolnshire and it meant a week spent with them and a week on the coast. This was the late twenties and early thirties, and we lived at that time in Leicester where Dad found work on the Great Central Railway. Mind you, to get to Cleethorpes then was hilarious. One route was via Lincoln, another route was via Boston. I can recall stations such as Dogdyke, Tattershall, Tumby Woodside and Woodhall Spa. It meant humping luggage (in boxes) and eagerly awaiting the pony and trap for transport. We've even been in the dark looking for each other with hurricane lamps. Dad and Mum travelled free, and the four of us at a quarter price.

On arrival at Cleethorpes we would be met by boys with trolleys who assisted us to our lodgings in Oole Road. We stayed with Mr and Mrs Hargreaves every year, because Dad said Oole Road was fairly central and handy. I was fascinated by Mr Hargreaves' motorbikes. He was always tinkering about with his 'Scott' and 'Indian' in the backyard. Mrs Hargreaves was known for her home-made pop and her cups of tea were out of this world. They both made us all most welcome. It was 1926 and I was eight years old.

At the end of Oole Road was a dilapidated building with many slates missing, and whilst out with my Dad he would stop, point to it,

Dentist Harry Ashling on an Indian motorcycle, registration number EE842.

and tell me it had taken a direct hit during the First World War, and many Canadians had been killed or wounded.

On a lighter side, Mum (who had shoulder-length hair) disappeared and returned an hour later with a 'Shingle' – a very severe haircut indeed, although fashionable at the time. We all saw Dad go berserk and we shot out of the way. 'It's a wonder you didn't go for the Eton crop and look like a man!' he said.

Some days whilst walking along the front with my brother we would hear a roar and a chugging and would see smoke and what looked like a lifeboat on wheels would pass us all. It proceeded along the promenade until it reached the slope to enable it to cut across the sands. Here it filled up with visitors and then headed for the sea. On reaching the water, the propeller took over and it was away. We all travelled in it during our stay. We thought it was marvellous.

On the other side of the road was a large building announcing 'The Fairy Caves'. Inside were wide channels with running water. Boats were in readiness and once in the water took over and off we went. There were myriads of lights, coves and grottoes. My brother and I always made our way there. It was three pence. Incidentally I used to have seven shillings to spend so I allotted four pence to spend in the morning, four pence in the afternoon and again at night. I can't recall whether there was a 'Figure of Eight' just then.

The greatest thrill we ever had in Cleethorpes was when we all went to the pier surroundings where 'Billy' was performing his ventriloquist act. We thought it was out of this world.

Our one disappointment was when we were on the sand – Dad with his four-cornered hankie – and we were allowed to go and paddle. The sea used to be so far out that we needed two hours to get our feet wet and often Dad would remark, 'You need a ruddy bike here!'

On the way back to our digs one day I was taken to the mine that stood on the front somewhere. Dad would give us some coppers to put in the slot and tell us how dangerous they were bobbing about in the sea and how just a touch would set them off. The money we put in went to a seamen's charity.

Tom Williams

Family ties

As a child, I used to go to Cleethorpes every year for my holidays. I clearly remember staying with Mrs Funnel at No. 131 Daubney Street. My favourite memory is of coming back for tea and seeing, there on the table, a three-tiered cake stand full of delicious cakes. I couldn't take my eyes off them and certainly didn't know which one to choose.

I am told that during the First World War my Grandma had a sweet shop in Barcroft Street. It is now just a private house but I would have loved to have seen it as it was then. In the same street there is the school where my mother, her sisters and brother went. We used to play in Sidney Park.

My uncle, who came from Barnsley, went to live in Grimsby where his father was a fisherman on the deep-sea trawlers that went to the Russian White Sea. My uncle worked on the railway as a fireman. He went to live in Cleethorpes with my great aunt after his father died. There he met my aunt and now they live in Leicester.

Pat Harvey

A false prediction

In 1960 we moved from Nottingham to Grimsby due to my father's failing health. He was advised to live in an area of cleaner, fresher air, somewhere where his lungs would not suffer the daily bombardment of smog and

Left: *Pat Harvey's Grandma had a sweet shop here during the First World War. Does anyone have a photo of the house as it was then?*

Below: *Barcroft Street flooded after a combination of heavy rain and high tide defeated the drainage system in 1933. As a result, a pumping station was built near Poplar Road. Third from left is eighteen-year-old Gladys Lockton (née Goodman), Pat Harvey's mother, who died in 1945.*

dirt. We had a good summer that first year. My father took us to Cleethorpes and we sat on the beach near the Boating Lake. My sisters and I had a great time digging and making sandcastles. My mother and father sat and watched and also enjoyed the sunshine. Late in the afternoon a gypsy came on to the sands and started approaching people telling them how lucky they were, etc. She approached my father and told him that he had been ill almost all his life suffering with many different illnesses. This was quite true. As far back as I can remember he had always suffered from bronchitis in the winter. She then told him that this was now all behind him and he would live to be ninety. Unfortunately, my father suffered a very bad bout of asthma and bronchitis the next winter and died the following April. This event has stayed in my mind all this time.

Sandra Leonard

Sandra and Karen Edwards with their cousin Keith Brown at Cleethorpes in 1949. One of the bridges over the Boating Lake is just visible to the right.

Visiting relatives

My memories of Cleethorpes began during the Second World War when we used to have regular family holidays staying with my grandparents, Mr and Mrs Tom Nangle, at No. 55 Crowhill Avenue. I also visited my aunt and uncle, May and Tom Chrome, who lived at No. 66 Sea View Street. Another uncle, Walter Motteshead, lived on Manchester Street, Grimsby, which was handy for him as he was a Grimsby Town supporter.

With all these relatives it may seem as though the family roots were in Cleethorpes but not so. Uncle Walter's surname points his and my mother's roots as west of the Pennines, whilst my father's roots were in Nottingham. It was my grandparents who moved the family to Cleethorpes, or rather my grandmother who, having lost her husband Peter Motteshead at an early age, married Tom Nangle and moved to Cleethorpes. Tom was a native.

Michael Allen

Often returning

My parents were married at Old Clee Church and for a while my father worked at Immingham, but this was in the 1920s and redundancy soon occurred. With no work locally, they moved to Nottingham where they spent the rest of their lives. In my mother's case, although she was happy enough, she always rued the day she left Cleethorpes behind. Needless to say, every opportunity to return was taken, whether it was for a long holiday or just a day trip. This is why I looked on Cleethorpes as my second home, and am fond of it still, even after travelling the world on various exotic holidays throughout my life.

My earliest memories were of Cleethorpes at war. Air raids were an almost nightly occurrence and, as there were no shelters nearby, the whole family took shelter under the stairs – all bar me as I was fascinated by the dogfights occurring overhead. My dad used to take me into the garden where we could see the searchlights sweeping the skies and the German bombers

August Bank Holiday 1956 saw the Ashton and Thompson families enjoying Cleethorpes' sun.

pounding the distant docks at both Grimsby and Hull. It was a sight and sound I will never forget. My ambition was to be a Spitfire pilot and get in amongst them. I remember the rumour at the time was that the German bombers used the dock tower as a marker and flew round it hitting the docks at will. This was why it was never touched by bombs.

Michael Allen

Spending on the 'slots'

When the war ended the task of restoring Cleethorpes began. The day Wonderland reopened was a dream come true for me. I used to head there every day if I could. The Big Dipper was my favourite but the many slot machine parlours also took a share of my pocket money. My daily route to the prom took me down the 'eight foot', as my grand-dad called it, to St Peter's Avenue, onward through the market place, then down the ramp

past the Royal Cinema, where Uncle Walter was projectionist, past the railway station entrance and on to the seafront. If my uncle had his window open, I used to call up to him and get a visit to the projection box for a while.

Michael Allen

New tastes

Once on the seafront my first call was at the new 'Meddocream' American whipped ice cream shop. This was the only place I knew that sold this confection and I often used to dream about it back home in Nottingham. Nowadays it's on sale everywhere but then it was the absolute in new tastes.

On other days I used to head for the Humberston end of the prom where the open-air swimming pool and the Boating Lake were. The pool was the biggest in the land I believe, and it sure took some effort to swim a length, although as it was oval I was never on course.

Sadly, this has long gone but not the Boating Lake. I was a regular on the rowing boats and had many a happy pirate game involving landing on the islands and marooning.

Just after the war, the other half of the pier was still standing, with a bosun's chair strung between the two halves. I believe the army used to occupy the outer half and pull themselves across, as duties demanded. Later on, of course, the far end of the pier was demolished leaving the short bit that remains today.

Michael Allen

Fish dishes

The members of my family who stayed in Cleethorpes were involved in the fishing industry. My Uncle Tom was a lumper on the docks and my cousin Walter was a mate on a trawler.

This meant that fish often featured in my diet and to this day I still visit Cleethorpes for a good fish dinner.

Michael Allen

The shy crab

There was one time when I went to Cleethorpes; I was just turning six years old. I went to the beach with my sister, nanna and granddad. We went for a picnic and we spotted a crab under the pier. My sister and I watched it for twenty minutes and it wasn't moving. We asked nanna and granddad if we could catch it, but they said no. They were sunbathing at the time.

So my sister and I went to the crab and picked it up. When it started wriggling its legs, we put it down quickly. Then it tried to climb

An unusual visitor to Cleethorpes beach draws a fascinated crowd.

51

up a pole under the pier. Believe it or not, it got one metre up the pier pole. We ran over to nanna and granddad and told them about the crab climbing up the pier pole. When we went back to see it again, it had gone.

Liam Chalder
(aged ten)

So much to enjoy

We usually avoided the resort on Bank Holidays as it was so crowded with hardly room to fill one's bucket and make a sand pie.

My friend and I had seen some children building castles near to the promenade and shouting to passers-by to 'throw down your odd halfpennies, please!' We thought it a good idea and followed suit, until my friend's mother saw us and was not at all impressed so we had to abandon our source of income.

Sheffield people seemed to favour Cleethorpes, and we were very intrigued by their accent and often remarked, 'Don't they talk funny?' They probably thought we did. There wasn't so much then in the way of entertainment, although I think Jimmy Slater had a concert party at one time.

I didn't go on the Big Dipper; it seemed a bit scary and very noisy. The donkeys were more in favour.

Cleethorpes has altered considerably since those days, but the happy memories will always remain.

Joyce Robinson

Gaynor Edwards at Cleethorpes in 1958. Note the beach huts in the background.

This roundabout near to the Big Dipper at Wonderland had a traditional air-driven fairground organ in the centre. Many visitors would pause there to enjoy the music.

Learning the hard way

I must have been about ten or so when I learnt one of the hardest lessons of life. Mum and I were spending a lovely day on Cleethorpes beach. It was one of those childhood days when the sun shone hot and bright all day. I had been building the usual sandcastle, and Mum must have decided I deserved an ice cream. She gave me half a crown and sent me to the kiosk about fifty yards away.

The ice cream must have cost about nine pence; it wasn't a straightforward amount. I paid my two and six and waited for the ice cream and the change. As she gave me the change, the kiosk owner looked at me strangely. I noticed it and it put me off. Several steps away from the kiosk I looked at the pile of mixed coins in my hand. It was sixpence short. I knew from the look she gave me that the woman had done it deliberately, and I also knew that she could easily browbeat a young kid and claim it had been a two shilling piece I had given her. I went back to my mother and she put the change into her purse without checking it.

Even at that young age, I thought how sad it was that people had to make their living so dishonestly. I wondered how many other people she gave short change to. It was many years before I wanted anything from a beach kiosk again. Even now, I am very careful what coins I give to such traders.

How sad that one kiosk owner, through petty greed, has damaged the reputation of all others, and taught one child a lesson in mistrust that has remained all these years. Once bitten...

Jeff Sandford

An illogical fear

When I was very small, I remember my parents taking me to Cleethorpes by train. When we came out of the station there were some flats and on the balcony of one was a small monkey on a chain. For some unknown reason, for it was well out of reach, I was very frightened of it and used to run past as fast as I could. It was unusual as I wasn't frightened of any other animal – well, the ones in the street anyway.

My mother said she was concerned as I used to go up to big dogs and hug them. I loved horses and donkeys, and always went up to stroke them, so why the monkey was so frightening I don't know. I probably grew out of my fright, or perhaps the monkey died.

Joyce Robinson

Staying with relatives

We Brights were a family of six: Mum, Dad, my elder brother John, my twin brother Derek, and my younger sister Irene. When we grew up in the mid-1950s money was tight, as our parents had just purchased their first brand-new house.

We used to visit my parents' friends who lived in Barcroft Street, Cleethorpes. They were known to us as Auntie Brenda and Uncle Roy (Mitchell) and they had a son called Michael who was younger than us. We used to travel from Leicester in a motorcycle combination and the journey in those days used to take nearly four hours.

All four children travelled in the sidecar, with the luggage in the 'nose' part. I remember when we were misbehaving that my mother, who was riding pillion would stand up on the footrests, open the roof to the sidecar, and whack us with her gauntlet gloves!

We came year after year to my aunt and uncle's house in Barcroft Street, which was a small terraced house. My uncle used to fash-

ion a bench out of a plank and cover it with an old blanket so that we all could sit at the dining room table. Where all the camp beds came from each year, I don't know, but all six of us were well looked after and fed for a week's holiday every year. Happy days! And, of course, the sun always shone.

Lynn Padmore

Cycle visits to Cleethorpes

As a young schoolboy, I used to spend many happy days during the long summer break with my aunt and uncle (Mr and Mrs B. Clarke) who in 1953 had just bought a newsagent's and tobacconist's at No. 54 Pasture Street, Grimsby. They had the shop for many years and made many friends, particularly Mr and Mrs John Skinn, when Mr Skinn was the Circulation Manager of the *Grimsby Evening Telegraph*.

On the shop's half-day closing we often cycled to Cleethorpes, pausing halfway for a rest and an ice cream. Uncle had a big old black 'carrier' bike. It advertised the *Grimsby Evening Telegraph* on the board under the crossbar, and had a big metal framework on the front to carry the newspapers. My aunt and I borrowed bikes from the Revell family who lived nearby.

Cleethorpes was a wonderful place to visit. Apart from having to walk such a long way across the sands to reach the sea, I can only remember hot sunny days and making sandcastles – these sort of pleasures, whilst so simple, were probably all anyone had in those days.

We always headed for the Winter Gardens end of Cleethorpes as aunty thought the other end was a bit 'tacky', but nevertheless the Big Dipper and the fun fair in Wonderland were huge attractions to me at that time, and I was allowed to spend my pocket money in the penny slot machines.

Ralph Walker

A sunny picture of the pier slipway, with Victoria Terrace and the station clock in the background. The postcard was sent on 21 November 1932 to Mrs Webster in Llandudno from her 'loving nephew and cousin Ben', who complained that it was foggy and raining!

Something for everyone!

Entertainment was provided by various beach attractions. Walking west from the half moon steps to the beach you first came to the Jimmy Slater Super Follies. Jimmy was a Cleethorpes man who lived into his nineties. I believe there were five men and five girls in his troupe. The sands were roped off from the stage to the wall of the promenade to accommodate paying customers sitting on deck chairs. Members of the audience on the promenade were caught by one of the girls with a collection box during the show.

Next on the beach was a chair-a-plane ride, then Charlie Joules' Singers. They sang the modern songs for sixpence a time. Then there were two helter-skelters, one double and one single, where, for a penny each, we could carry a mat up the stairs and slide round and down until we hit the sand at the bottom.

Hancock's amusement arcade was on the beach, raised up on legs of stilts. The Jolly Boats was a carousel where, for a copper or two, we could sit facing each other in a make-believe boat, as it conveyed us round in an up-and-down movement resembling the motions of a boat. As well as the ha'penny and penny slot machines, there was a pianola fitted with a pin cylinder which played a tune and moved the keys of the pianola up and down in conjunction with the music.

Walking west from the station there was a road from the promenade and the footpath (as there is now). This housed various attractions including Brown's Rock Stall, which sold rock made in the factory at the rear. Prices began at a penny a stick, but they sold a bag containing rock of many sizes and colours with 'Cleethorpes stamped all the way through!' as the sellers would cry.

Jugs of tea with thick cups were on sale to take on to the sands for picnics. A sixpence deposit was charged, returnable when the crockery was returned.

'Wonderland', further west, was a large entertainment complex, housing various rides such as the Dodgems, The Ghost Train, The Glass Maze, and numerous games. During the Second World War it was converted into a Jeep assembly factory, and is now a Sunday market.

In the High Street at the top of Isaac's Hill was Humpheries' dress shop. In the holiday season a rail was placed at the front of the shop exhibiting bathing costumes, priced sixpence. These costumes stretched on contact with salt water and it was funny to watch people emerging from the tide with their costumes hanging down to their knees!

Iris Morton

Baggy costume

My swimming costume was knitted in bright stripes of orange, blue and green. I remember it clearly; it was quite jazzy and smart until it was wet, but then it was another story. The sagging was a sight to behold!

Jean Ashling

Eating at the seaside

We spent quite a lot of time at Cleethorpes, and the first thing we did was buy a stick of rock with 'Cleethorpes' all the way through it. The penny ones were mint flavoured and pink, but if you were well off and had tuppence, you had a choice of three flavours.

We used to suck them to a point but they were hard on the teeth, which made them quite a lethal weapon and very useful if you met any enemies.

Another interest was to watch the making of 'sea foam candy'. The machine appeared to be a large empty bowl with an electric whisk going round. The candy just seemed to appear from nowhere. I expect there was some kind of sugar substance lining the bowl but it was all very mysterious to a young child. The people selling it used to wrap it round a stick. I think it cost 2d. The trouble was it wasn't very secure and after a few licks would finish up in the sand which didn't do much for the flavour. The same happened with sandwiches on the beach. It was mostly a choice of having egg and sand or cheese and sand.

Joyce Robinson

Holidaying in the thirties

Our holidays in Cleethorpes during the thirties were put on hold by the war. Our first landlady was Mrs Moore and later we went to stay with Mrs Tattersall, whose husband was

A sight to behold! Jean Ashling wearing a knitted bathing costume that had suffered in the water.

on the fishing boats. I can remember him coming in from the trawlers in the mornings. Both these boarding houses were in streets off Kingsway. We used to walk down Kingsway to the Bathing Pool. There were gardens all the way. Each little plot had different features in them. One I remember had a little boy holding up a Wellington boot, with water coming out of a hole in the foot of the boot. Ross Castle had a walkway sloping down and round it to the bottom that took us to the seafront.

My mother used to go to the shops first thing in the morning to buy chops and other meat as well as vegetables to take back to our landlady ready for her to cook for our dinners. It was the usual thing and my dad also brought some of his home-grown peas and potatoes from home. I remember seeing on the bill for the week the item 'Cruet' with a charge of 6d.

We watched the singing parties on the sands and went to the shows on the pier.

There was also a man who made lovely pictures in the sand every day. I remember thinking it was a shame that the tide took them away.

The *News Chronicle* had a good publicity stunt. A reporter visited seaside resorts to give away prizes. He carried a copy of the newspaper, and members of the public had to carry the same newspaper and challenge him. His 'name' was Lobby Lud, and he became a national institution. Dad always carried the newspaper, 'just in case'.

Mrs B. Morley

Spanning the years

During my school days in the 1930s, Dad and Mum always took my sisters and me to Cleethorpes for a week's holiday. We always stayed with a dear old lady named Mrs Booty

The Beyless family and others, sitting under the pier in 1923 or 1924. From the left is Harriet (neé Withers), with young Leonard and Albert in front of her. Second from right is Arthur Albert Beyless. Others were acquaintances from the boarding house. With thanks to Sylvia Grant (Beyless granddaughter).

at No. 4 Pelham Road. My mum bought the food which Mrs Booty cooked for us.

I remember that on occasional nights Mum and Dad went out and my elder sister and I were allowed to stay up. We played a game of rummy with Mrs Booty.

If Mum had to go shopping in the daytime, Dad would take my sister Edna and I across the main road to a playground and leave us there for a while. That wouldn't be possible these days. We used to go on the beach opposite the railway station and there would be a small stage and somebody singing. One song I especially remember was *Carolina Moon*. The person running the show came round selling broaches in the shape of a small moon and Dad bought us one.

One day Dad took Edna and me on a walk across the sand and we were cut off by the sea. I think it was some fishermen that got us back.

Then came the Second World War. I began work at fourteen years old – the day war was declared. After that we had two weeks' holiday at Blackpool.

In 1945 I married George while he was still in the Royal Navy. He was on a minesweeper, HMS *Prowess*, and they had to enter Grimsby Docks with engine trouble.

We have had a run through Cleethorpes and Grimsby this year. My memories are still there.

Mrs M. Frost

Economising

We always stayed at Cleethorpes, and went sort of 'self-catering'. We bought our food and our landlady cooked it for us back at the digs. We stayed with Mrs Kempster each year.

One year when my parents went, my mother saw a blue dog figure, costing 2s 6d. Dad said, 'If we economise, we might be able to buy it.' They did and she bought it.

Sylvia Grant

Holidays in 1939

Our August Bank Holiday to Cleethorpes in 1939 started off not at all well. My mother, fourteen-year-old brother and I (at that time nearly twelve) were to travel by bus, commencing very, very late at night – probably near midnight.

The journey was a nightmare as I suspect that there was a fault with the vehicle's exhaust. Certainly before we had been on the road for an hour, many passengers were being violently ill. One man in particular looked as though he was dying. I held on until the journey was nearly over but then the lack of sleep and the stench of vomit caused me to dry retch. There was another call of, 'Stop the bus, driver!'

It was past dawn when we arrived and the first thing to be done was pinpoint our digs. I think that Mum provided our breakfast and tea food and at midday we ate our food on the beach. Breakfast was a fry-up and tea was bread, butter and jam. Mum and we two boys shared one double bed. We were not well-off.

That first afternoon we two boys were on the beach with Mum when she said that she was going to get some items for tea, 'and that lady [nearby] will give you the written address of the digs.' Both of us had been so tired after the journey that we had no idea where the digs were, although we had been there. An hour passed and then my brother said, 'I've got the address, Norman, come on.' I finished what I had been doing, looked up and found my brother had gone and the lady who had been given our address was nowhere to be seen. The beach was packed with people, so there was no chance of spotting her. I nearly panicked, but then I thought that I could probably remember part of the way we came. I left the beach, crossed the beach road and after a few minutes came to what I think today was a narrow walk through. There I stood for over an hour getting more and more anxious, as dozens and dozens of people brushed past me. Eventually my brother's voice said, 'Where have you been? We are waiting tea for you. You always spoil things.' I could have hit him, but he would have hit me back. After settling in, I found that our digs were managed by a young couple, in their late twenties. They had a little girl of about four years old.

On the beach we found the 'Super Follies', a typical seaside show. One of the refrains I remember went like this:

Life begins with Super Follies
When the busy day is done.
We don't care how much you work us,
Just as long as we have fun.
Georgie and Tommy are a couple of lads,
They keep us smiling
– it's always best to keep on smiling.
Life begins with Super Follies
When the busy day is done.

We bought a photo of those long-gone Follies. They were very good singers, dancers and comedians. Once a week they held an amateur talent show, when children would do a turn and the audience applause would decide the winner. My brother, who sang in clubs, went up and he outshone the other boys and girls. The first prize of a canteen of cutlery was in the bag until a little blind girl went up and recited a poem about the house she would one day have. She got the sympathy vote and the canteen of cutlery. My brother won a small square camera which we had for years although it was never used.

Once a week the Follies had a Gala Night when the men dressed as ladies and the ladies as men. The stage was on the beach and usually had seats for the paying audience. The 'do it on the cheap' audience leaned on the railings and saw the show without paying, moving

This location is described as the Children's Corner (Southend) Cleethorpes. The youth standing next to the posters on the left has in fact climbed onto his bike to peer into the Bathing Pool. The registration number on the car is EE 70?8. What a pity the railings are in the way! This postcard was franked on 28 July 1931 at Crosby in Scunthorpe.

Lincolnshire Road Car Company's yard with excursion buses, early 1950s.

away only when the collecting bags came round. However, on Gala Nights canvas screens were put round the stage so that only the seated customers could see the show.

With the Follies show over, we would move a few yards and watch the sand artist, then move along and watch the magician. One of his tricks was to put razor blades into his mouth and take a long drink of water, then put a piece of thread into his mouth. After a long pause he would pull the end of the thread and out it would come with the razor blades tied to it. Still going along the beach, we came upon a *Punch and Judy*-type box. On the backcloth was stitched a doll's headless body, the head being the operator's head poking through the backcloth. He operated the doll's arms and legs with his own hidden hands. So by simply moving along the beach, a whole morning's entertainment could be had for free.

Using a cheap 'sea line fishing kit' (a line and a hook – that's your lot!), my brother cast the hook into a breakwater pool and pulled out a

young eel. This drew admirers from all over the beach. We had a photo of the event, and I often wonder where that photo is now.

I had a go on a game which was a set of clock dials, each having a fast-moving sweep hand. The idea was that the competitor who could press his button and stop the hand closest to the six, won. I won, but what was the prize? It was a big stick of rock. That was nearly as good as my brother's eel!

A friend of Mum's and her two sons were at Cleethorpes with us. Mrs Brown was a big woman, and I mean BIG. While sitting on the sand we saw that the sea was coming in. We all got up to move back – except Mrs Brown who couldn't get up on her own. We all gathered round her and tried to help by pushing and shoving. This set her off laughing, and the more we struggled to get her up the more she laughed. Eventually we did get her on to her feet but it was a close run thing!

At the end of the week we left for home. The newspapers were full of the submarine

The Kingsway Hotel in its early days.

Thetis tragedy. My older sister who had holidayed at Portsmouth had gone on a day trip to France but they were not allowed ashore as the French Army was mobilising. A month later, on 3 September, war was declared.

After I was married in 1952, we went to Cleethorpes. It was awful, though we did see the 'Wall of Death' motorcyclists and then a five-legged donkey.

In 1982 we motored over from Mablethorpe. Things had improved though the crowds did not materialise. A despondent shopkeeper blamed 'a useless council'! What a shame! Cleethorpes in 1939 knocked Skegness into a cocked hat. Wake up, Cleethorpes, you can do it again!

Norman Hastings

Happy days!

I am eighty-eight years old and my family went to Cleethorpes for holidays in the summer. We had an apartment but used to buy our own food. The lady we stayed with used to cook it for us. She provided potatoes for the week, and charged 1s 6d for the use of the cruet. These were put on the bill at the end of the week.

Do you remember the large jug and bowl in the bedroom? There was cold water for washing but a small jug of hot water for men for shaving.

I remember Billy the ventriloquist. People used to sit in deckchairs in a circle and enjoy his shows. After his show, he had children up on the stage for competitions. One was a race to eat a stick of rock, and the winner received a prize. Once, he had them eat an onion. Tears were rolling down their cheeks – simple fun! While everybody was enjoying it, his wife would come round with a little black bag saying, 'Please, lovely people.'

On the sands was a helter-skelter. One penny paid for a mat and a good ride down. The 'Jolly Boats' went round and round and up and down. It was like being on waves. There were bicycles fastened together, and they also went round and round. That ride cost 3d. My sister and I loved it.

Nearer the Kingsway we looked down on the sands that never dried out. People made lovely pictures in the sand and shouted, 'Throw a penny down, please!' I noticed this year that tons and tons of sand have made this a lovely beach.

I also saw the new leisure centre, the little train and the gardens. There were always lovely gardens, and the Boy with the Leaking Boot.

When I was sixteen years old, my late husband was my boyfriend then. We went with four other people on our bicycles to Cleethorpes. It took us eight hours! We had a 'snap' taken sitting on one of the guns that was on the promenade.

We had simple pleasures, like having a halfpenny cornet each day. When we went for a paddle, we did not wear a bathing costume. We just tucked our frock and underskirts into our knickers. We would be content to play in the sands all day. We were very happy, not like the kids of today who I hear crying, 'I want, I want… ' and, 'I'm bored!'

Mary Bailey

4 Attractions of the Area

'Those were the days, my friend…'

During the 1930s, the Humberston Fitties welcomed us for around six weeks every summer during the school holidays. Family friends lent their bungalow to us – father, mother, my sister and me. It was very comfortable by 1930s standards – with a spacious lounge, three bedrooms and a kitchen. There was no running water, refrigerator, electricity or indoor toilet. The latter was located 100 yards away from the bungalow, in the sand hills. Night visits were by torchlight as we trekked out one by one, disturbing all the rabbits which had come out to play.

All our friends and relatives visited us at some time during the six-week period. One day Grandma, who was visiting us, got 'latched in' the lavatory and only when we espied a white handkerchief fluttering through the six-inch space above the door did we realise where she was spending… her time!

Once a week on a Friday, the night soil cart came round to collect and return the metal containers. Friends were discouraged from visiting as the week wore on, for obvious reasons. Oil lamps provided the light for us, which had to be shared by alarmingly huge moths. Water was at a premium, so large enamel jugs and metal milk churns were taken by car to the spring to be filled. This was a good distance away from our bungalow and, if we ran short, emergency supplies had to be fetched along the half mile on foot if father was at the surgery in Cleethorpes and no car was available. We used to meet up with other families at the spring so the water fetching was not considered a chore.

The late Sid Burton, the photographer, and his family owned a bungalow much further along from us and we often used to gather there. Apart from the fact that they were happy and amusing family friends, they had a large swing in their plot and owned shuttlecocks and quoits. Sid's son Rowland and his friends built a boat one summer and many of us gathered for the official launching ceremony. The community spirit was wonderful as large groups came together for various events – bonfires and fireworks, etc.

Always with adults, we walked out to the creek which was quite deep, and indulged in what was called 'dab-sticking'. A long pole with prongs attached to a bar at one end was prodded in front as we walked along and the resultant catch was welcomed as a free meal.

We were all sad as the summer holiday came to an end but rejoiced to know that the following year we would be back. It was from Humberston that we hastened home in 1939 as the storm clouds of war appeared. Thus ended a way of life. I feel so privileged to have experienced that decade.

Jean Ashling

Left: *Jean Ashling on the swing at their Fitties chalet. The 'shed' on the left is the toilet where Grandma was 'latched in' until she could attract a rescuer.*

Below: *The Burton's chalet on the Fitties where the Ashling family enjoyed summers in the 1930s.*

A Catch! 'Dabbing' in the sea at Humberston in the 1930s. The home-made 'dab-stick' can be seen, and Jean looks pleased as her catch is transferred to the basket.

The thrill of the Lancaster

I remember the time at Waltham Windmill when the Battle of Britain Flight flew over. In the museum there was a special exhibition about the RAF and the Lancaster bombers.

There were lots of activities outside, including a bouncy castle and many stalls. The main attraction seemed to be the Lancaster bomber flying over, bringing much pleasure to the crowd. Cameras were flashing and video cameras were whirring, and everyone was shouting because of the noise of the engines.

The Lancaster made one final circuit and then flew away into the distance, as if it had never come. We could hear its engines slowly and steadily fading away.

James Nunn
(aged ten)

65

Jean and Mrs Ashling collecting water half-a-mile away from their chalet. A milk churn would hold at least two gallons.

Photo boosted Windmill funds

On the way to my Scout's meeting one very dark November night, Dad and I caught sight of the floodlit Waltham Windmill. After dropping me off, Dad went home for his camera and took some photographs. Several weeks later Paul Needham, a member of the Waltham Windmill Preservation Society, said they were looking for a new postcard to sell to raise funds. Dad showed the photos he had taken and Paul borrowed one to take to the committee. They must have liked it, because a thousand were printed and put on sale at the mill and in the village, though they didn't mention the photographer. However, the *Grimsby Telegraph* included a print and the story in one of its issues.

Chris Leonard

Donkey rides on the beach

The donkeys were brought down to the beach by means of a railed board (donkey steps) and

'Waltham Windmill at night', which was produced as a postcard.

the owners hired boys or girls to run behind them and hit their rumps with a stick to make them run for the riders. These children were known as 'donkey wallopers'. There were no restrictions as to the weight the donkeys carried, and although they were well looked-after, I am sure the days were too long for them and some of the plump ladies they carried were a heavy burden.

Iris Morton

Enjoying the countryside

As a teenager I had a lot of fun with my friends who attended Grimsby's Flottergate Methodist Church. We would often cycle to Humberstone, Dona Nook or Immingham when the weather was reasonable. Once we visited a farm at Immingham and I drove a tractor in a field for the first and only time in my life.

John D. Beasley

Boats with wheels

My mother took me to see a children's concert on the pier. I wasn't very thrilled with the show, but what did impress me was the scene that greeted me on the sands below. The tide was fully up and there were many motorboats plying for business. One was tied to the landing stage attached to the pier

The 'walloper' appears to be restraining these donkeys so that Lynn and Irene Bright can have their photograph taken about 1957.

Children of the Springfield Methodist Church Sunday School on their outing to North Somercoates in 1964.

slipway, and another was using a home-made landing stage. This was a long gangplank attached to two large wheels at the seaward end and two small wheels at the other. Two men wearing waders were holding the boat to the gangplank while passengers clambered aboard the boat.

What really caught my eye were four motor-boats mounted on wheels. When they were fully laden they drove into the sea and when the water was deep enough the propeller took over propulsion from the wheels. These amphibious vehicles usually plied for trade on the sands opposite the railway station. When the tide was out people had a long ride on the sands and a much shorter sea trip. Many years later I was given a lot of transport cuttings and amongst them was one about the ships with wheels. They were built on a Ford lorry chassis and were called 'floating charabancs'.

Cleethorpes was the first resort to use them. The earliest one dated from 1925. As far I know none survived the war.

In the early post-war years two former US army amphibious six-wheel vehicles were used on similar duties.

Norman Drewry

Riding the rides!

The exciting feeling inside me was like fizzy pop. The gorgeous smell of burgers and fries, and the screaming of the girls made me feel more confident about going on the rides.

On our visit to Pleasure Island, the first ride I went on was The Magic Carpet – it was brilliant! It gave me butterflies in my stomach. Next I went on the Condor, but my Dad chickened out. It went up and up, making me

Many people enjoyed their visits to the zoo at Cleethorpes. Opened in 1965, it closed twelve years later. Ray Leonard is seen here trying to coax an animal out of its enclosure in 1967. The area later became Pleasure Island.

feel dizzy. We also went on the Crazy Loop, the Break Dancer and then the water slide.

We had our dinner; it was gorgeous. Afterwards we went on another selection of rides, but my favourite was the Crazy Loop.

Sam Crookes
(aged ten)

Sunday evenings at Wonderland

In the mid to late 1950s some members of the church youth club would go to Cleethorpes on a Sunday evening by the No. 6 bus which went via Weelsby Road. We would walk along the promenade to Wonderland and in those days there was a wonderful assortment of amusements available for the visitors. At the very end was the Big Dipper. Inside its space

Known as the 'Figure of Eight Railway' when this old postcard was produced, the Big Dipper was a favourite attraction for many years. What were the five people in the foreground doing, just posing for the camera?

The Boating Lake. The area of trees (left) became the site of the Discovery Centre.

was a motorboat pond, and on the ground, running under the Big Dipper tracks themselves, was a miniature railway. That was an exciting ride with the Big Dipper thundering and rattling overhead. The owners of that land had packed three attractions into a very tight space. The area now gives little clue to the delights of those attractions. None of us was officially 'courting', but it was our chance to size up the opposite sex and see whom we fancied the most.

David Bradley

Overheard

I was walking around the Boating Lake and noticed two lads fooling about in a canoe. The inevitable happened. The canoe tipped over and the lads were thrown into the water. As they climbed out of the lake I heard one say, 'I hope you have an auntie who lives in Cleethorpes!'

Norman Drewry

Bunny's Place

A former bowling alley and bingo hall were converted into an upmarket venue for live entertainment by former trawler skipper Bunny Newton. Opened in May 1975, it cost £250,000 to build and could seat 1,000 people. The star of the first show was Frankie Howard. I wanted to go but couldn't get tickets; they had all sold out. Later I worked there for a while, and the group I remember best was the Hollies; they were very good.

One singer who refused to come was Shirley Bassey. They said she wanted £25,000, a share of the box office takings and a big orchestra. Perhaps she didn't really want to visit Cleethorpes.

Bunny's Place was sold on 23 May 1979, later being renamed Peppers and Shakers nightclub.

It burnt down in 1982 – a sad ending for a top-flight attraction that Cleethorpes so needed for visitors and residents alike.

Stephanie Bennett

Cleethorpes' Airstrip

For a few years in the 1950s Cleethorpes possessed an airstrip. It was on a sandbank which ran beside the Boating Lake. Two Auster aircraft used it to give pleasure flights. Usually they took off in a southerly direction and flew around the forts and along the centre of the river to give views of the shipping, then back along the coast. When not in use the aircraft were kept at Waltham airfield. An old caravan was used as a booking office and a former US Army Jeep was used to warn people who strayed across the airstrip. It also towed the caravan to safety when the tide came in. Air traffic control was limited to the driver of the Jeep giving visual signs to the pilot, and navigation warnings came by GPO messenger delivering a telegram.

John Hewson

Flying from Cleethorpes

We had a family holiday at Cleethorpes in around 1958 or '59. My brother and I flew for the first time in an Auster aircraft from the beach towards Humberston. The Austers were built in my home area of Leicester. I think the fare was five shillings for each flight. Later on, the family we stayed with won a large sum on the football pools.

Paul Williamson

Dancing at Cleethorpes

Soon after my friend Stuart completed his National Service with the RAF, we discussed the matter of enlarging our social circle – in

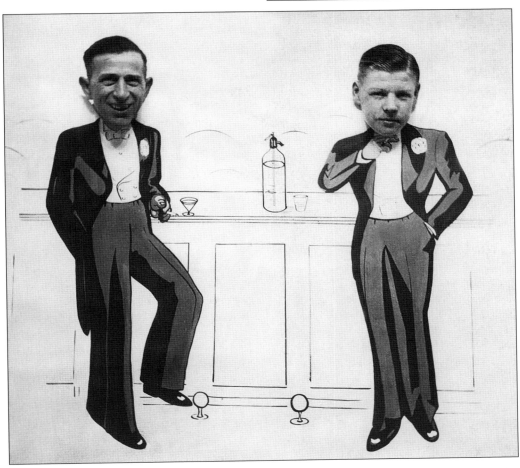

Two dapper young men at the bar. Herbert Bradley and Gordon Smith, photographed by Jollysnaps at Wonderland.

other words, meeting more girls. It was agreed that ballroom dancing was the answer. Accordingly we enrolled at Jimmy Stevenson's School of Dancing, attending two evenings at his beginners' classes, held in the upper room of the Sussex Recreation Ground Pavilion. Jimmy had a successful formation team and competition dancers, but it soon became apparent that we were unlikely candidates. We had neither the co-ordination or the rhythm, let alone the desire to dress up as numbered penguins!

After the lessons there was a period of free dancing, records being played without any announcement, and it was up to us learners to decide what sort of dance it was. I could tell a waltz from a tango, just. Stuart had some difficulty, so he devised his own way of telling what dance was being played. If all the dancers got up it was a quickstep, if half got up it was a waltz, if about a quarter danced it was a foxtrot and if only three couples got up it was a tango. Both of us avoided the foxtrot and tango. After attending two of the school's dances at the Winter Gardens where we danced to the music of Wally Fryer's Stricttempo Orchestra, live instead of his records, we felt we were ready to go to public dances. We started by going to the pier, where we regularly danced with two girls; one was a very good dancer and could avoid my size tens and Stuart's size nine-and-a-half shoes quite nimbly, but it was very difficult to have a conversation with her. However, her friend was more outgoing but a less skilful dancer.

When the summer season ended we transferred to the Café Dansant. At that time it was in a poor state of decoration and repair, though it was always crowded. It had been used to billet troops during the war. To protect them should the glass roof shatter during a bombing raid, a wooden frame covered with fine-mesh aviary wire was suspended from the roof. The roof leaked and fire buckets were hung from the wooden framework.

Memories of the café spring to mind. On an Easter Saturday it was so crowded the doors were closed and latecomers turned away. In the café, ladies out-numbered the men about two to one. Across the road at the Winter Gardens the ratio was the opposite. New Year's Eve 1952 found Stuart and I at the café. Shortly before midnight, the band walked out and the dancers were instructed to follow the band. The band walked towards the Bathing Pool then turned, went down the promenade and back on to Kingsway, then halted at the door of the café when they ceased playing. Their timing was good; we then heard the sirens of shipping in the river welcoming the New Year in. The band resumed playing, and we followed them back inside and danced for another hour. Later the café was closed for some months for repairs and redecoration, and although it was very smart, by this point it had lost its popularity. Those of us who went over to the Winter Gardens during its closure remained there.

Norman Drewry

Out of season

Once, on an outing with the school, we paddled out to Haile Sand Fort and waved to some men who were stationed there.

On the way back, I filled my bucket with cockles only to be told by my mother that they were out of season so they were dispatched down the outside sink, no doubt to join their brothers and sisters in the Humber.

Joyce Robinson

Getting rid...

On one of our trips on the Humber paddle steamer, our landlady, who had accompanied us, wore a hat which she said she had never liked. She wanted to be rid of it so decided to throw it overboard. As she threw it, the wind blew it on to the deck below. A passenger there thought it had blown away accidentally and brought it back to her!

Mary Barker

Attractions to visit

Between 1918 and 1939 my mother was very friendly with Madame Drury who was a music teacher living at No. 139 Thrunscoe Road, Cleethorpes. As a result we visited Cleethorpes from Grimsby every fortnight or so, and I played with her children Joan and Peter.

I can clearly remember the open-air Bathing Pool being opened and I swam there regularly in spite of the cold weather. I remember falling off the huge Bukta ball and splitting my swimming trunks. I also recall the Boating Lake extension being built at its Cleethorpes' end, and walking past the Leaking Boot on the way to the Winter Gardens where we later danced regularly.

As a Boy Scout, I regularly went with the other boys to swim in the sea-water swimming baths situated on the promenade side of the market place. Then we went into the market-place to eat fish, chips and peas. I remember seeing the Wonderland amusement arcade expand from a small place to what it is now. I frequently visited the Grotto café near to Ross Castle.

Terry Nundy

On beach and sea

Cleethorpes boasted the first amphibious boats, used as a beach attraction. These were the size and shape of a lifeboat and held twenty to thirty people. They were designed to run on the flat sand on enclosed wheels, but when driven into the sea a propeller was used.

Iris Morton

Sunday afternoon walks

During the winter period, several of us took a walk at Cleethorpes. Meeting at the Bathing Pool we would walk around the Boating Lake and have a coffee in the Birds Nest Café, then meet some more friends and walk along the promenade to Steel's Café in the market place for a toasted teacake.

Jenny Bagley (left) and Anne Spence on the beach at Cleethorpes in 1967, enjoying the traditional attraction of the seaside.

Doreen Ashton playing in the sandpit near the Boating Lake in 1938.

Sometimes we would visit the hockey pitch just beyond the pumping station. On asking who was playing, some joker told us it was hospital staff versus hospital out patients. From then on we always supported the losing side with calls of 'Come on, out patients!'

Once my friend Dave was walking very stiff-legged. On being asked about his injury, he replied that he had purchased some tape which Woolworth's claimed would put permanent creases in trousers. What they hadn't said was that it made walking and sitting down very difficult.

We met two friends, one pushing the other in a wheelchair, who claimed he had injured his foot at football. Later we met them again,

coming back in the opposite direction. This time the injured party was pushing the wheelchair. They admitted that they had borrowed Grandma's wheelchair hoping it would bring attention from young ladies. Up to then they had been unsuccessful!

Usually there were very few other people walking along the promenade but occasionally a bright Sunday afternoon would bring out a few walkers. One of our party would go over to the railings and point out to sea. We would join him and gaze and point. When a small crowd had gathered also looking out to sea, we would walk away, leaving them trying to see what had attracted our attention. Of course there was nothing unusual to see!

When the summer season started our Sunday afternoon walks ceased.

Norman Drewry

Unique clock on display

One day in 1952, I was walking through the gardens near the pier. I was pleasantly surprised to see a clock on display that I had seen in Battersea Park funfair the year before. I believe it was called the Toucan and had been built to advertise a certain company. On it were various items that opened, moved and performed after the clock had finished striking the hour. It was on a tour of the country, and I often wonder what happened to it when that tour finished.

David Bradley

The Biggest Ever

The annual hospital carnival was known as 'The Biggest Ever'. The floats came along Grimsby Road past my father's dental practice. Upstairs, the front room was a surgery with a huge bay window. My father would open the

On the right is 'Bumper Mumby' a regular character in Cleethorpes Carnival Parade during the 1930s, and winner of first prize in 1934. With him is Florence Andrews who lived in Park Street for many years. After she died her dress was donated to Normanby Hall, and the hat, wig and cape were given to a Hull theatre.

An A.B.C. Theatre

RITZ - CLEETHORPES

Manager : W. J. CONOLLY   Telephone : 61713

DICKIE VALENTINE
AND BIG SUPPORTING COMPANY

Programme Threepence

A night not to be missed! Dickie Valentine was at the height of his popularity in 1956 when this show began a week's run at the Ritz from 20 August. Six other acts supported him, including 'Radio and TV's comedy stars' Morecambe and Wise.

window and place a cushion on the sill for me to sit on. My father, the nurse, the patient and I would then watch the spectacle pass by. The exciting part for me was when the men on stilts held up long poles, to which were attached long tubes of hessian or canvas with a ring at the top to hold the tube open. These were to collect the money from all the folk who were watching from their bedroom windows. Hardly a window was unoccupied along the whole route which eventually ended, I believe, at People's Park in Grimsby. I still remember

sitting on that window sill and Nurse Hanson holding on to my dress at the back 'just in case!'

Jean Ashling

A much-missed attraction

My aunt used to tell me about the opening of the Ritz in 1937, on 31 July. The entrance had been filled with flowers and lit by lovely hanging chandeliers. It had a Crompton theatre organ that people loved to hear played during the intervals. Aunt used to talk of Noel Briggs as the organist. One of the usherettes she got to know was Violet Balderson, who had previously worked at the Lyric in Victoria Street, Grimsby.

The Ritz was one of the biggest places in the area and was able to stage large shows and concerts. It was in a good position to attract visitors, and hosted the local Boy Scout Gang Shows for several years. It became the ABC in 1956 and finally closed in November 1982.

Stephanie Bennett

A beautiful sight

One day in 1937 or '38, my mother took me to Cleethorpes without giving any reason. When we arrived close to the pier entrance I was surprised by the number of people standing on or around the pier. There was an air of expectancy and excitement and then there was a cry of, 'Here it comes!' There was a roar of aircraft engines, and then the most beautiful sight I had ever seen. A four-engined flying boat dipped down over the pier, banked and then climbed away.

Martyn Leonard admiring a 1936 Coventry Eagle at the Hawerby Park rally of old vehicles in 1984. The motorcycle was bought in a very rusty state and rebuilt by its owner, B.W. Chapman of Fulstow.

HAWERBY PARK RALLY

SPECIAL ROAD LOCOMOTIVE

FOR HEAVY HAULAGE PURPOSES

14th – 15th JUNE 1980

30P

A Hawerby Park Rally brochure from 1980. Similar gatherings still attract large crowds at different venues in the area.

No longer did I want to be a train driver or bus conductor when I grew up, but a flying boat pilot. When the war came and all my friends wanted to be Spitfire pilots, I remained loyal to the flying boat and wanted to become a pilot of a Sunderland flying boat, the military version of the Empire flying boat I had seen at Cleethorpes.

While serving with the RAF in Egypt in 1948, I took a holiday in Luxor and had the pleasure of seeing an Empire flying boat land on the River Nile. I never did get to realise my dream of piloting one.

The only flight I had with the RAF was when I was stationed at RAF Lyneham in 1947. I flew as a passenger in a York transport aircraft to view the terrible bomb damage in the Ruhr Valley.

Norman Drewry

Saved from the tide

One year our neighbours, a couple with a little boy, decided to come with us on holiday. They hired a fold-up pram for the week. One afternoon we all went for a walk on the beach while the tide was out. While we were there enjoying ourselves, the tide turned so we began our way back. Suddenly we saw the pram was beginning to float out to Spurn! Luckily Mr Brown was able to retrieve it. The little boy now has a grown-up family of his own.

Mary Barker

Two penny sandwich and a penny cornet

When I was very young I thought it unfair that adults had ice cream sandwiches costing two pence and children were only allowed cornets costing one penny. When my mother took me to Cleethorpes she usually bought me an ice cream cornet. On one occasion, the tide came in bringing a very cold wind with it. I was shivering with cold so my mother wrapped my scarf round me and said that we should hurry home. I thought as my mother was being very kind to me this was the time to ask for a two penny sandwich, and was very disappointed when she said it was far too cold for any ice cream.

Joyce Robinson

5 The Pier

A Century of Progress

When the present pavilion was built in 1905, it could be used only in the summer because of the lack of heating. After this problem was resolved, the pavilion was able to open all year round. In the 1930s, dancing took place every evening and most afternoons, to 'a modern dance band'. Some might be surprised to learn that, despite pre-war Sundays having a reputation for being boring, dances were held then just like any other day of the week. Concerts were also popular – a 'Programme of Music' was staged in the afternoon at 3 p.m. and in the evening at 7.45 p.m. on Sunday 27 September 1936.

During the early years of the Second World War, there was much fear of a possible invasion by German forces. Someone in authority felt that piers were an ideal place where troops could land. Personally, I would have thought that a secluded bay would be a more likely option. The order therefore went out for east coast piers to be breached. Thus it was that a section of Cleethorpes Pier beyond the pavilion was forcibly removed, and the long pier neck left isolated, at the mercy of the sea and storms.

After the war ended, there was an opportunity to restore the pier, as there was at many other resorts. Indeed the government offered compensation to Cleethorpes Council, the pier owners, as it was they who had insisted on the structure being sectioned on security grounds.

However, the sum suggested was not sufficient for a full rebuild. An extra £26,000 would need to be raised from the Council's coffers. Sadly, they decided against spending the additional money. The long-isolated pier neck was demolished in 1949, with 200 tons of salvaged timber being used to help build a new stand at Leicester City Football Club's Filbert Street ground. The remaining timber went to Wonderland, with nearly 300 tons of metal going for re-smelting.

By the 1960s, the British seaside was largely not what it used to be. Instead of going for a week or a fortnight at Cleethorpes, holiday-makers could journey to the Costa Brava or the Seychelles.

Not surprisingly, the pier suffered. A series of summer shows were not popular, and Cleethorpes Council decided to cut its losses by putting the structure up for sale.

Unfortunately, the new owners, Funworld Ltd of Skegness, were unable to make the pier pay again. By 1983 it was closed and padlocked. The Council were given the option of buying back the pier, but declined after it was estimated that restoration could cost £200,000.

Yet, despite fears that Cleethorpes would lose its pier, local businessman and club owner Mark Mayer purchased the structure on 24 July 1985. £300,000 was spent on con-

The pier and pavilion. A postcard sent from No. 34 Albert Road, Cleethorpes, to Mr Jas Schofield of No. 197 Chapel Road, Hollinwood, on 27 August 1911.

verting the pavilion into a modern nightclub, which opened that September as Pier 39.

Tim Mickleburgh
Chairman, National Piers Society

Changes

The pier in the early days stretched over the promenade and continued over the Submarine public house, hence its title. A turnstile at the entrance led you either onto the pier for two pence, or a penny admitted you to the pier gardens.

First on the pier was the main hall used for dancing, and then there was a long walk to the café at the end. In around 1936 the walkway over the public house and promenade was removed during a modernisation period and the railings enclosing the gardens were removed. The start of the Second World War and the invasion scare saw the removal of part

of the central section, cutting the café off from any access. The café burned down for reasons unknown and after the war that end of the pier was demolished.

Iris Morton

The showboat saga

In the 1950s, the truncated Cleethorpes Pier became involved in the saga of what was intended to be an offshore entertainment showboat.

The boat was meant to be anchored by the seven-mile limit near Haile Fort. In the interim we had to dig an area 100 feet long, 30 feet deep and 15 feet wide. This was at the side of the breakwater near the pier, with me being the banksman organising it. When the tide came in, the ship was supposed to be pulled here.

Alas, the tug towing the boat had problems and steel ropes had to be placed around its

A J.F. Lawrence postcard of Ross Castle and the pier. The 'castle' was named after Edward Ross, secretary of the Manchester, Sheffield & Lincolnshire Railway, which was responsible for popularising Cleethorpes as a holiday venue. Close examination of the beach beyond the pier will reveal what appears to be a boat.

pilings to shackle the vessel, which had originally been brought from Sheerness in Kent, as a business proposition. The excavator succeeded in pulling it several yards, and we used wooden railway sleepers to help in reaching the breakwater site.

People used to walk on the pier to view the stranded ship, and the Chairman of Cleethorpes Council – which ran the pier – served the owners a summons after three months to have the boat removed.

John Coulam

Fire on pier

On 29 June 1903 a fire broke out on the pier and the concert hall burnt down. This dramatic event affected the attendance at nearby Bursar Street School. More than seventy children were absent in the afternoon to watch the fire. The present pavilion was built in 1905.

From Bursar Street School archives

Later developments

I moved to this area in 1969, and well remember seeing Cleethorpes Pier for the first time. It was short like Redcar Pier, due to having been blown up in the Second World War as an anti-invasion precaution. The Pier Pavilion had been modernised in 1968 at a cost of £50,000, and now had sixty seats for concerts, pantomimes, bingo and wrestling. An annual coin, stamp and postcard fair was held there in 1971, 1972 and 1973, so I was able to buy postcards of piers, on a pier! The fair later transferred to the Winter Gardens. The dealers came from all over the North and Midlands, but the only dealer from this area was Brooklands Collections of Sea View Street.

In 1975 there was a small fire in the pavilion, but worse was to come in 1978, when, on 11 January, high winds battered the east coast of England causing much damage to seaside piers. Most of Skegness Pier was washed away and Hunstanton Pier went completely. On Cleethorpes Pier, 150 handicapped and elderly people were trapped in the pavilion for two hours when heavy seas crashed through the wooden decking of the pier. They were eventually rescued by police, coastguards and off-duty firemen.

The pier was soon repaired, and in 1981 it was sold to Funworld Ltd, an amusement company from Skegness, for £55,000. This company turned the Pier Pavilion into an amusement arcade and roller-skating rink, and in 1982 ran a summer show, which turned out to be a financial disaster.

The pier was closed in 1985. Mark Mayer (1949-1994), a businessman and nightclub owner, bought it and made it into a nightclub and bar. It was renamed Pier 39 after a San Francisco pier which had been converted from a rundown steamer pier on a forty-five-acre site to make a market place of 100 shops, boutiques and restaurants. Our Pier 39 was re-opened on 4 September 1985 by the Mayor of Cleethorpes. It was sold to Whitegate Leisure Plc, later Northern Leisure, in 1989. The nightclub was renamed Excess at Pier 39 and a walkway was added to shelter customers in 1993.

In 1998, part of it was renamed The Paradise Club. In July 2000, Viking FM Radio held a live concert on the pier attracting 4,000 people who watched from the beach and promenade.

The National Piers Society visited the pier in 2001, following its Annual General Meeting in Grimsby.

Lester Kitching

Wet feet at the concert

Several of us attended a concert at the Pier Pavilion. There was an usually high tide that evening and the sea was splashing through the decking of the pier. The audience sat through the concert with wet feet!

Joyce Robinson

Visiting the pier

When I was a child, my parents owned a hardware and ironmongery shop in Grimsby. Most of the goods were supplied by Bradley Brothers of Hull. After making his deliveries to our shop, the driver sometimes took my sisters and me for a ride to Cleethorpes Pier in his van. We did not have a car at this time so these visits were exciting and much anticipated.

John D. Beasley

This postcard was sent to Mrs Miller of No. 52 Trafford Street, Scunthorpe, by Georgina on 9 November 1911. The English is not perfect but reads, 'We arrived safely after a struggle with the slog we had a grand time at thorpes [sic] yesterday. Fred wants to go every day until he starts school.'

6 Education

Camping at the YMCA

During the 1970s, the YMCA camp at Humberston was available to Humberside schools to have an open-air activity week. The camp had four wooden huts that could accommodate about eighty-four children and four adults, a dining room, a sports hall and showers. There was ample room outside for games, and a small swimming pool about three feet deep. This pool had been the water reservoir when the camp had been used for training during the war.

When it was a bit cold to swim for long, our teacher used to throw coins into the water to encourage us to have a splash about. I collected twenty-seven pence and spent it at the tuck shop. The warden, Mr Hargraves, had planted some fast-growing conifers around the pool to give it some protection from the biting east-coast wind, but it was still cold!

There were treasure hunts around the caravan camp and along Anthony's Bank Road. We had to find answers that were often names of caravans, or spot half-hidden signs. It was an observation test and it made us look closely at things.

We visited the parish church in Humberston, St Peter's. The vicar showed us around and explained the different parts. I had never been inside a church before, and I didn't know what to expect. It was very interesting, but very cold despite the sun shining outside. One afternoon we walked to Cleethorpes Leisure Centre and enjoyed a swim in the pool. Some of the public visitors were put out that so many children (about eighty) were in the pool at the same time, but it is open to all.

Once, our teams joined in a tug-o-war knockout contest. Twenty of us pulled on one end of the long rope while another team pulled on the other end. As soon as we began to put our full force on it, the rope snapped in the middle and we all fell over. The teacher laughed and said, 'It wasn't supposed to do that!' We all thought it was funny, too.

The year my sister went they took the school tents. One lad complained in the morning that somebody had been up in the night poking him in the back. The teachers took it seriously and warned everyone to be more considerate. No one owned up to doing it – then we discovered what had happened. We moved the tents each day to a fresh piece of grass, and under the tent where the boy had been sleeping was a new molehill. The mole must have tried to throw the soil up and wriggled against the boy's back. We didn't know who to feel more sorry for!

The teacher in charge had slept all week in an old caravan. On our last morning all eighty-odd of us woke him up early by banging pans and buckets and shouting outside the caravan. He came to the door all sleepy and looking very annoyed – but then he laughed! None of the other teachers could keep a straight face either. One of them must have tipped him off. He was in on the joke and it was all a lot of fun.

Later the YMCA camp changed its name to the Tertia Trust, and specialised in holidays for disabled people.

Maureen Thompson

Not just the caretaker

In 1902 Mr John Ingoldby was engaged as a caretaker and occupied the Bursar Street School house. He was allowed free rent, rates and house coal, and given a wage of £60 a year. A small extra allowance was paid for serving children's dinners. He was affectionately known as 'Daddy Ingoldby'. He would boil eggs, roast potatoes and brew tea on the heat-

ing system, and would feed a needy child if necessary.

From Bursar Street School archives

Dropped from the team

I was at a Cleethorpes Comprehensive School in the seventies and played in the school football team. I wasn't the best player, but good enough to help the forwards score the goals. I enjoyed the matches and made some good friends. Then Terry came to our school. He was a brilliant player. They dropped me to let him play. The games teacher said they needed the strongest team to win the league. He said I should still go to the matches in case someone was ill and to show my loyalty.

After a few weeks I still hadn't had a game, and a team outside school asked me if I would

Children from Grange Middle School, Grimsby, ready to 'Heave!' at the YMCA camp, Humberston.

Having a GOOD TIME at

Y.M.C.A. Youth Camp

HUMBERSTON Near Cleethorpes

The YMCA camp postcard, showing the pool, sports hall and field.

play for them. They weren't as good as the school team, but they were very friendly and made me very welcome. After six months Terry moved schools again, and the games teacher wanted me to go back. I refused because I didn't like being used, and I didn't feel I could play for two teams. The players in my new team were much fairer and we enjoyed playing the game without wanting to be 'the best' all the time. The games teacher didn't like it when I said I couldn't play for both teams. He said I should 'chuck' the new side because they were 'rubbish'. I couldn't do that.

Ian Jackson

At school eighty years ago

My school was on Welholme Road. I was there from 1917 to 1924. The head teacher was Miss Jones. We sat two to a desk and used wooden pens with nibs, complete with blotting paper and inkwells. We had a building in the playground where we went for cookery and laundry lessons. We entered music festivals in Hull, and on the pier at Cleethorpes.

Three girls in the class were called 'five-to-four' girls, as they were allowed to leave class at that time to get to the level crossing to catch the train. Their home was in Waltham.

I have happy memories too of the carrier coming every Friday from Tetney full of farm produce and lovely golden farm butter. Cleethorpes was always known by the locals as 'Meggies'. I never knew why. I was fourteen when I left school in 1924. I received a very good education.

Mrs E. Barson

Illness at Bursar Street School

Minor outbreaks of infectious diseases such as mumps, measles and chickenpox have occurred

Football championship winners of 1903/4, Bursar Street School.

The village school at the corner of Kirkgate and Cheapside, Waltham, next to the Methodist church. New bungalows now occupy this site.

at various times to affect the school attendance, but influenza has been the most prevalent disease. In July 1918, more than a quarter of the children were absent due to influenza, so the school was closed for twelve days.

By December of the same year, the disease became so widespread that the school was closed until further notice, only 169 children being present out of a possible 330 in the girls' department.

In 1927 the school was closed for a fortnight due to an influenza epidemic, and yet again in 1954 when 207 children were absent out of a total of 810.

From Bursar Street School archives

'Coming for a paddle, Sir?'

In the 1980s, certain Grimsby schools held a holiday play club during the six-week summer break. I was often the leader-in-charge for one of the weeks. On the Wednesday of each week, buses would take the 120 or so children for a day out at Anthony's Bank. There were several reasons for going there. It was a short bus journey away; there was a café and toilets; there were swing boats and trampolines; the sand was smooth and clean and the area was easy to supervise. The children would play on the beach, enjoy their huge packed lunches, and finally go home exhausted. One year when we arrived, we noticed a difference to the area. The swing boats and trampolines had gone, and the sand looked darker and wetter. Still, the café was open, and the toilets, thankfully. As soon as they arrived, the children were running about on the beach, while we leaders established a base on the steps to oversee their activities. I went for a walk on to the sand and chatted to the children. Soon their shoes and socks were off so that they could paddle in the pools of water and splash each other. They were thoroughly enjoying themselves, but I had my doubts. I was looking at the sand.

Children of Eastfield Junior School, Immingham, working at Keelby on a topic that compared the two communities and their facilities. These houses in St Bartholomew's Close were built as single-storey cottages during the seventeenth century. The end wall clearly shows how an extra floor was added in brick later.

A group of them came up and said, 'Come on, sir, aren't you going to take your shoes and socks off and come for a paddle with us?' 'No, no, I won't, thank you,' I said.

'Oh sir, come on, it's great.' Their enthusiasm was infectious, but I was still dubious, looking at the sand. They persisted, and I continued to refuse. Finally I had to say, 'No, I won't. And I don't think you should either.' 'Why not, sir? Come on, sir! It's fun.' So I had to say, 'Have you seen what you are treading in? That brown stuff!'

They looked down at their feet, and the look of growing realisation on their faces was a joy to watch. Their understanding became vocal and almost in chorus they exclaimed, 'Yeeuuk!!!' and raised dripping feet from the water. They washed their feet in some clean water, dried them and put their socks and shoes back on.

Fortunately a year or so later, the new sewage treatment works came on line and only pure water was then being pumped into the Humber. Never again did the sand have its brown covering, but the grasses that now grow on that section of beach seem to have a vigour all of their own!

Gary Carson

Post-war baby boom

By 1955 the total school population had risen to 1,200. The junior school's share of this was 890 – the highest recorded in the school's history. There were nineteen classes. It was not possible to have an assembly as the whole school could not fit into the hall. It had been partitioned to form two classrooms. Therefore the playground was used during fine weather.

From Bursar Street School archives

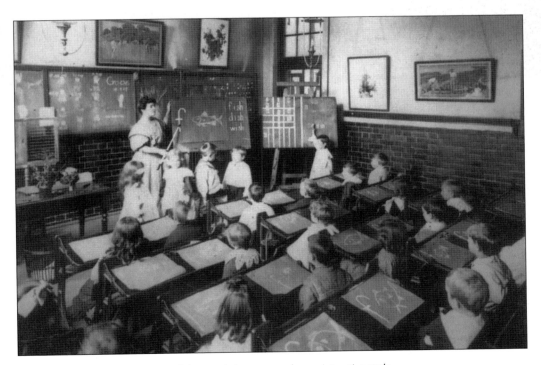

This classroom from the early years of the twentieth century makes an interesting study.

The village school

I remember the head teacher of Peaks Lane School, Mr Southcott, particularly because his family lodged with us for a while when he first took up his post. His wife was also a teacher, and they had a daughter, Gillian. Where is she now, I wonder? Mr Southcott was followed by Mr Garton. I remember the outside toilets there. They were emptied into the 'stink cart' which came to the village each week. Many houses had to be serviced in a similar way, though we had our own 'sump'. There was of course electricity, but we had our own well from which we pumped water, a weekly job for Dad.

A friend and I used the New Waltham village school playing field for our cricket matches – one player each side! Also we went fishing for newts in the pool of a market gardener, and for fish in the beck running along the edge of the field near Peaks Lane.

Revd Roy Allison

Rapid growth

Bursar Street Schools were opened on 1 September 1902, having cost £10,000 to build. There were 436 children on roll; Miss Cleathero had charge of 149 girls, Mr Kirman had 223 boys, and Miss Burton had 64 in the infants. In 1904 the school population had doubled to 876 pupils.

From Bursar Street School archives

Bursar Street School. The ladies staff of 1952.

A Bursar Street classroom in 1907. In the centre, second from the front is Dorothy Cooper, later to become Mrs Harry Ashling.

7 Sport and Leisure

Soccer Club that always plays 'away'

There is no one still alive who can remember Grimsby Town's first game at Blundell Park, Cleethorpes. It was played on 2 September 1899 against Luton, and the score was 3–3.

Pre-match entertainment and that put on during the half-time interval has varied greatly over the years. A long-haired folk singer, complete with electric guitar, did the business in the club's dark days of the seventies.

In recent years, stars of the local professional pantomime have been introduced to the

Harrington Street runs at the back of Blundell Park, and became very congested on match days. A visiting supporters' coach, 215 CML, stands with private cars double parked in places. Over the fence, trains also wait for the match to end before returning with away fans.

crowd. Last season (2001/2) Alvin Stardust was the big name.

Isolated incidents stand out in the memory. In the sixties a thunderball of a shot from big Ron Cockerill flew past the Pontoon stand goal and knocked out a youngster in the crowd. Thankfully he recovered after treatment.

Still as popular as ever down Blundell Park way is wee Dave Boylen, a mainstay of the Lawrie McMenemy Fourth Division championship-winning side of 1972. Late in the 2001/2 season, when the Mariners were in serious trouble and likely to drop into Division Two, he was cheerleader before games and really got the crowd going.

None of the 22,484-strong crowd present will ever forget the 3-0 win on 2 May 1972 that clinched the Division Four title. Remarkably, when this fixture was first played earlier in the season, fog came in off the Humber and the match was abandoned after just eighteen minutes.

Sadly missed at Blundell Park these days is local journalist and broadcaster, Charles Ekberg. Stories about 'our Charles' are legendary: He once incurred the wrath of manager Alan Buckley by leaving the press box and running to the manager's bench to check the name of a town goal scorer – during the game!

On another occasion, when his language was a darker shade of blue, he did not realise that his Radio Humberside microphone was still on!

John Kirkby

Enjoying the swings

Living on the Nunsthorpe estate in the 1940s and '50s, our nearest recreation ground was Barrett's, just off Scartho Road. During school terms this was visited quite often to play on the swings and slide. The summer holidays were a time to be more adventurous, so my pals and I

would make our way to the Sussex Recreation Ground, as there were more attractions.

I remember especially the suspended ropes with large metal hoops attached at the bottom end, which we were able to swing on. The rings were about five feet off the ground but I was not very tall, so I found it a little difficult to get on them. I had to hope somebody would help me. Because of this I did not go on them very often. While there we would talk and play with other boys whom we did not know. There was no fighting, no rivalry, just children playing in harmony.

David Bradley

Not good sailors!

In July 1955 a Humber Swim was included in Cleethorpes carnival week. The yacht club provided dinghies and pilots to ferry the swimmers across to Spurn Point. Sadly, some of the would-be swimmers had not sufficient experience of the Humber swell and were seasick on the crossing to Spurn!

Doug Wise

Visiting Blundell Park

I was a regular Grimsby Town supporter in the 1950s. I would stand with my father and uncles in the open corner between the Main and Pontoon stands, in all sorts of weather. We used our bicycles to get there and left them at one of the houses in Hart Street. The house owner charged us one penny each for the use of his front garden and got to know his regulars. By using the same house each time, we could guarantee that at the end of the game our bikes would be ready at the gate for us.

David Bradley

More than just sand at Cleethorpes

According to the late Jack Oslear, when he joined Cleethorpes Cricket Club in 1922, its ground was situated at the end of Sherburn Street, where the school playing fields are now located. In 1929 the club was warned of the danger of losing the ground because of council plans for building a housing estate. Fortunately at that time, the tenancy of a piece of land, which was later expanded to become the present ground, became available. It was rented for £25 a year from John Hardy, and later Mr Tom Fletcher, owners of Hardy's Farm, the western side of which became the site of Signhills Junior School. A meeting of members was held in Gray's Rooms on Alexandra Road to discuss ways of financing the move. Ten members donated £25 each to the fund. Among the vice presidents of the day were 'Uncle' Jimmy Fish, G.T. Baker and Arnold Beardsall. There was only one access to the ground, a cinder track, now Hardy's Road. The nearest houses were in Signhills Avenue and two on King's Road, which became the Cromwell banqueting suite and 'Summerfields' Flats. One of the club's earliest County representatives was Wilf Gillow in 1926. He played for Grimsby Town FC at that time and later became manager.

Howard Swain

Early years

Norman Maslin joined the club in 1931 when the captain was Wilf Wilson, who in the 1960s presented the H.W. Wilson Cup for the championship of the Lincolnshire County Cricket League. The first home match to be played on the new ground was against Scunthorpe Town on 13 June 1931, which the visitors won.

The club played in Division One of the Grimsby and District Cricket League, when there were only five other teams, namely Grimsby Town, Scunthorpe Town, the Amateurs, Appleby Frodingham and the LNER friendly fixtures were also played, and during the Second World War opposition came from the army, navy and air force sides. It was not until after the war that Sunday cricket was introduced and the club reverted to a friendly fixture list until the 1960s. In 1948, the club provided two wicketkeepers for the county. Brooke Armitage was the regular, and Les Bennett from the Second XI deputised.

One group of people who cannot be praised too highly from those early years until the 1970s was the ladies committee. Not only were they renowned for their lunches and teas, but they also helped raise valuable income for the club.

Howard Swain

Facilites expand

It is very difficult for present club members to visualise that small ground of the early 1950s; the dilapidated wooden pavilion, tiny changing rooms with splinter-giving seats, and the score box perched precariously above the gents' toilets. The development of the town of Cleethorpes prompted expansion. Houses were fast-engulfing the ground and the move to preserve the future of cricket had to be made. Thanks to the wise counsel and influential help of Jack Oslear, Norman Maslin and Alderman Albert Cox, the present eight acres were purchased from Sidney Sussex College for what may now appear as a paltry sum in 1955, safeguarding the land for recreational purposes instead of the intended residential development. Secretary Tim Holt and groundsman Wally Shepherd made significant contributions in the years that followed.

In 1963 the new pavilion was opened. Social functions necessitated a larger lounge and the elevating of the dressing rooms, built in 1971.

A tense moment at the Sidney Park Bowling Club. Third from the left at the back is John T. Cooper, granddad of Jean Ashling.

In 1978 two squash courts (Cleethorpes' first) were opened and 200 new faces entered the club's life.

Howard Swain

Playing success

1967 saw us win the league for the first time, having entered three years earlier. In 1968 during Norman Maslin's year as County President, the American Cricket Association played the Lincolnshire side at Cleethorpes. The follow-ing year the first minor county match was played on the ground against Staffordshire. 9 August 1970, that unforgettable Sunday, brought the International Cavaliers, a galaxy of legendary cricket names, and 3,000 spectators, to the ground.

In 1980, Cleethorpes was chosen as the venue for Nottinghamshire to play their first ever first-class home fixture out of the county, against Worcestershire. Also in the 1980s, Middlesex were the visitors in a Sunday League game, and Sri Lanka played twice on consec-utive tours. Benefit matches have been held for

Children sailing their boats on Sidney Park lake in 1959.

Richard Hadlee, David Gower, Alan Lamb, and a joint one for Jim Love and John Birch. July 1995 saw another memorable game on the ground, the Sunday League match between Nottinghamshire and Yorkshire before a capacity crown and a delighted club treasurer.

In 1957 Ray Mawer took over the captaincy, a position he held for ten years and the club emerged from being a good local team into one of the area's leading sides, regularly supplying players to the county team. 'The main reason for this upsurge', says Ray, 'was the emergence of the youthful talents of Bob Leafe, Roy Oslear, Howard Swain and David Maslin and their transition into first-class club

cricketers; Paul Gregory and John Sunley into fully-fledged county players, and Martin Maslin into one of the finest amateur cricketers most of us have seen'. The spirit was great and confidence grew. The foundation was set and, up to 1983, Cleethorpes won the Lincolnshire County Cricket League Championship eleven times. In 1975, Don Oslear was appointed to the first-class umpires' list and in 1980 to the Test panel. He went on to officiate in five Tests.

In 1981, the club made its first venture into the John Haig Trophy with great success. The regional final was reached, away at Scarborough, and on the way the notable scalps of York and Bradford were taken. Yorkshire League clubs began to realise that there was more than just sand at Cleethorpes!

From 1984, a new chapter in the club's history had opened; fresh faces, new friends and, nationally, a higher standard of cricket. Needless to say, championships and cup wins became elusive. In 1988, to give the club a much-needed boost, a professional was engaged for the first time.

Like most cricket clubs, tours have played their part over the years. After Devon in 1952 and 1953, tours took the team to Hampshire, the Isle of Wight, Essex, Norwich, Kent and Newcastle.

Priority has always been to produce a playing area of the highest standard possible. The constant upkeep of the pavilion has made it a club to be proud of and the number of people who attend functions is proof of that. Work is in hand to add a third squash court, refurbish the cricket changing rooms and improve the clubroom.

The club has come a long way since the 1920s and each succeeding generation has built on the foundations laid by its predecessor. Let us hope the present tenants continue this enviable tradition.

These items were prepared by Howard Swain who played from 1957 to 1997. Howard holds the club record for the aggregate number of wickets of over 1,500.

8 Difficult Times

The coming of war

In 1938, at the time of the Munich crisis, my father joined the Auxiliary Fire Service. During the school summer holidays in 1939 my mother took me for a day at Mablethorpe. We travelled in a Walmsley Brothers' new Dennis coach. I remember she took me into an amusement arcade and many people were gathered round a stall and were listening to a radio. I asked her why they were all so interested, and she said that people thought there might be a war. One day in the summer of 1939, I was walking home from school for dinner when I saw a Corporation bus with ARP (Air Raid Precautions) showing on its destination screen. This more than anything else brought home to me that war was coming.

Norman Drewry

Bad winter

One particular memory is of the bad winter of 1946-7, when New Waltham was cut off for three days. I think the railway line was open, though my father returned home late by train one evening having been snowed in for several hours.

Revd Roy Allison

Taking chances

We lads used to go on the promenade at Brighton Street slipway and climb through the rolls of barbed wire on the sea wall. We would see how far we could go without getting our clothing caught. The soldiers used to chase us off. We would also go onto the sand hills in front of the Boating Lake. There were trenches all over and many wooden 'ack-ack' gun placements. Again the soldiers always chased us off.

Near the pier, we would watch an Army plane land on the sands and take off again. I believe it was a Lysander. We also watched soldiers cross the gap in the pier on a cradle to reach the lookout post at the end of the pier.

Alf Evardson

Being evacuated

My grandfather said that three of his daughters and his grandchildren should be evacuated when the war began. Accordingly, arrangements were made for us to stay with some old family friends at Tealby near Market Rasen. They had farmed at Laceby and had gone into semi-retirement to a bungalow with a smallholding.

On Saturday 2 September 1939, I stood with my mother, Auntie Jessie, my cousin Shirley, Auntie Joyce, Gyp the cocker spaniel, several suitcases and our gas masks outside my grandparents' house, waiting for the 11 a.m. departure from Cleethorpes of Lincolnshire Road Car's bus service to Lincoln. The bus arrived more or less on time, and was not far off being full already, there being only a few vacant seats at the rear of the bus.

At Brighowgate bus station the bus became full to capacity and my cousin and I had to sit on our mothers' knees. The bus on this particular journey diverted from the main route to serve the village of Hatcliffe. As we were about to return to the main road we spotted a little Morris car. The lady driver was waving to us. It was Marie, the daughter of our distant hosts. She had evidently been sent to fetch us. How all of us and our suitcases and gas masks could have fitted into such a tiny car is impossible to judge!

When we arrived at Tealby, there was the problem of getting off the bus. The gangway was blocked with standing passengers and luggage. The conductor had the solution. He got off the bus and opened the emergency door at the rear. He lifted us children down and helped the ladies to jump down.

At the bungalow, the adults had a conference. The building was clearly too small for us all. It was decided that my mother and I should go with Marie to stay with her on her farm at Kingerby near Market Rasen.

The next Sunday, war was declared. That night I was awakened by voices. I asked my mother what was the matter and she said nothing was wrong. The grandfather clock chiming must have woken me. The next morning I found out that the noise I had heard was the air-raid warden calling round to tell us that there was an air-raid warning. The only way to notify the remote farms around Tealby was for the warden to come round on his bicycle. By the time he had got back to his post, the 'All clear' had been given and he had to start his long cycle ride round the farms again!

Norman Drewry

Billeted soldiers killed

During the First World War, the 3rd Battalion of the Manchester Regiment was billeted in the Baptist chapel on Alexandra Road. During the night of 9 April 1916 and prior to the men being drafted to France, a bomb dropped by a German Zeppelin hit the chapel and killed thirty-one soldiers. There is a memorial to this event in Cleethorpes' cemetery, where they are buried together in a mass grave. The grave is still maintained by a Mr Peter Stacey of Lavender Court.

Iris Morton

Flood aftermath

I saw some of the devastation caused by the floods of 1953 along Suggitt's Lane. There were some garden sheds marooned in the street, and the road itself was ankle-deep in sand. The railway lines leading to the station were torn up, and looked as if a giant hand had twisted them into strange shapes.

Doug Wise

Early air raids

At first we had a few air-raid warnings both at night and during the day, but no actual raids. The Germans attacked the shipping during the day and laid mines at night. Seaplanes were used at first to lay the mines by landing on the sea, but this could only be done when the weather was clear and the sea calm. Later they dropped the mines by parachute, though some came down on land instead of in the sea. Once, a bus driver, with a bus full of airmen returning to North Cotes, saw a mine hanging by its parachute from a telephone pole.

Norman Drewry

Hearing the sound of disaster

Recent events often trigger memories of others that happened years ago. On 16 April 2001, I was standing outside my back door in Waltham when a distant bang shook the house. From inside, my wife said, 'What was that? It sounded like a crash.'

I replied, 'It sounded like Flixborough over again.' I hoped I was wrong, but casual remarks have a habit of including elements of truth.

My mind went back to that bright, hot afternoon of Saturday 1 June 1974. I had been crossing Kensington Place in Scartho, Grimsby, going to help a neighbour whose central heating oil tank was leaking. Halfway across the road I had heard a long, distant rumbling sound, not at all like thunder. A chemical plant at Flixborough had exploded over thirty miles away. In that disaster, twenty-eight people had been killed.

This time an explosion had occurred at the Killingholme refinery of Conoco, six miles away. I dread to think what it would have sounded like if it had been another Flixborough.

Tony Griffiths

New Waltham wireless station

My mother and I used to visit a friend at Scartho for afternoon tea. I enjoyed these visits as they entailed a bus ride. We caught the 3 p.m. bus from Cleethorpes in Hainton Avenue and travelled via Wintringham Road to Brighowgate where the conductor visited an ivy-covered cottage to pick up parcels from the agent. These were the days before the bus station was built. On reaching Scartho village we parted company; the bus went on to Lincoln. My mother and I walked though the churchyard to the friend's house. One day in early 1934, after tea the husband took me into his garden and pointed out flames in the sky.

He explained that one of the wooden wireless poles at New Waltham had caught fire due to lightning and had been burning for several days.

Later the wooden poles were replaced by steel ones and fitted with red warning lights. They could be seen from miles away. During the war they were lit only when aircraft were taking off or landing from nearby airfields. Local people always knew when our bombers were due to go on raids.

Norman Drewry

Polio outbreak

My earliest memories of Cleethorpes are very vague, but I do remember playing in the sand hills just past the Bathing Pool. I remember we were never allowed to go in the Bathing Pool as it was an open-air one and vulnerable to all weathers and diseases. This proved to be true when, in the 1960s, an outbreak of polio occurred and it was thought to have emanated from the Bathing Pool.

Sandra Leonard

A dangerous load

A friend of mine took his trolley onto the sands and found a rather large bomb. He put it on his trolley and covered it with his coat, intending taking it home, near to High Cliff. A policeman saw him and asked what was on the trolley. He uncovered it and immediately evacuated the whole area. The bomb could have exploded at any time!

We used to go looking for the butterfly bombs that had been dropped there. We had been told in school never to touch them.

Alf Evardson

Houses commandeered

The soldiers of the Second World War were billeted in commandeered houses on the Kingsway, between Brighton Street Slipway and the Winter Gardens. Furniture was removed as well as the occupants. The soldiers were nicknamed 'Koylis', from their regimental name, The King's Own Yorkshire Light Infantry.

Iris Morton

Serving in the GTC

I joined the Cleethorpes Girls' Training Corps in 1942 after leaving school at sixteen. We met at Reynolds Street School, on a Wednesday night, in the playground for drill if it was fine but inside the senior girls' side if it was wet.

Sergeant Major Charlie Collins of the Home Guard put us through our drill, but if we were in a procession the following Saturday, an officer from one of the regiments stationed in Cleethorpes came and gave his comments on our drill. One of the highlights for me was a trip to the dock for a visit up the Dock Tower. One of our officers (our CO) was courting a naval officer and he had obtained permission for us to go down one Sunday afternoon. We took the trolleybus from Reynolds Street to the Royal Hotel, then marched through the docks to the tower. We went up to the top in the lift. What a view it was from there: Hull and the Yorkshire coast, the barrage balloons on the river, and Pelham's Pillar near Caistor.

Another memorable visit was to North Cotes aerodrome of Coastal Command. This was another Sunday afternoon visit. I remem-

Cleethorpes Girls' Training Corps in 1942 at South Parade School, Grimsby. Joyce Humberstone has an arrow above her in the back row.

Pelham's Pillar at Fonaby Top near Caistor. Standing 128 feet high, it was erected in 1849 to commemorate the planting of 12.5 million trees by the Earl of Yarborough.

ber it was winter. We were all in macs and wellington boots as there had been snow over the weekend. We caught Walmsley's bus to North Cotes village and marched down to the aerodrome. We watched the planes landing back after a sortie; the squadron had just been issued with Beaufighters, a twin-engined fighter plane. We enjoyed our tea in the officers' mess.

We took part in Spitfire Week, Warships Week and processions through Grimsby and Cleethorpes. We always tried to march behind the Salvation Army band as they played some good marching music.

Joyce Tyson (nee Humberstone)

Cleethorpes at war

During the Second World War, Grimsby and Cleethorpes were made restricted areas, and therefore no visitors were allowed in the towns. You could be in the two towns only if you either worked or lived there. During the war there was very little to attract visitors to Cleethorpes. The north promenade was closed and later in the war Wonderland became a factory for assembling US Army vehicles.

The pier had a gap made in it to prevent it being used as a landing stage by invaders. A school friend claimed he saw it being blown up. A breeches-buoy was erected to allow men to get to the isolated part. People were not allowed on the beach and barbed wire was laid along the promenade. Empty shops and houses, the Café Dansant and Olympia amusement hall (later to become the Winter Gardens after the war) were all used for billeting troops. An anti-aircraft battery was stationed between the Boating Lake and the sea wall. A Lysander aircraft towing a target would fly up and down the seafront for seamen to practise with their Lewis guns.

The paddle steamer *Killingholme* sailed up and down the Humber as a tender to the barges

anchored in the middle of the river flying barrage balloons. These were to protect the shipping from low-flying bombers. The *Killingholme* had an interesting career. Built in 1912, one first duty was to carry HM King George V and Queen Mary around Immingham Docks at its opening. In 1916 it was used as a seaplane carrier. It would anchor on the Dogger Bank, awaiting German Zeppelins. Attacked by armed German trawlers, it suffered damage and its crew were injured. It returned to its duties on the Humber ferry until replaced by the then new PS *Lincoln Castle* in 1940, when it became a barrage balloon tender. It was scrapped in 1945.

Norman Drewry

Blocking the roads

When the invasion was expected, the authorities had trenches dug in fields to prevent German aircraft and gliders from landing. Signposts were removed and town names were painted over to confuse any Germans who landed. Buses showed route numbers but no destinations. In 1940 concrete gun emplacements were built all over, especially along the coast, and many pillboxes were built along the seafront. Across the main roads concrete barriers were erected which were about six feet high and four feet thick. An opening on the footpath allowed one pedestrian to walk through at a time, and on the road was a gap for one vehicle to pass through. In case of invasion the gap was blocked by inserting steel girders into holes drilled in the ground.

One Sunday morning I was cycling to Cleethorpes and found the Home Guard had placed the girders into the holes at the barrier in Clee Road, and in true *Dads' Army* fashion were having problems lifting them out. A bus was waiting to pass and the driver was becoming very cross. One of the Home Guard soldiers was my schoolteacher and I looked forward to telling my friends at school next morning!

Norman Drewry

Growing up during the war

I was born on 8 August 1932 in Grimsby, but went to live in Cleethorpes at the age of eight. I went to St Peter's Church School between 1940 and 1944.

Because the war was on, we all had to carry our gas masks all the time. On the way to school we searched the gutters for bomb shrapnel. Sometimes it was quite warm and very jagged. It soon wore out our pocket linings. We swapped it at playtimes. I do wish I had kept some.

On running to school our gas mask boxes became quite tatty. We used to get new ones from a shop in Cambridge Street that was an air-raid precautions station.

If the air-raid warning siren went when we were at school, we would all be herded into the air-raid shelter in the playground. All the children were given a large sugar candy stick to suck. We sucked it until it was like glass, but could not bite it.

When the all-clear sounded we all went back into school and carried on with our lesson.

Alf Evardson

No chicken for us

When we lived in St Peter's Avenue, a bomb dropped in Chapman's Field at the bottom of our street (George Street). It was a very large field full of chickens. Frank Broddle was in charge at the time; he later became Mayor of Cleethorpes. We children went looking for some of the chickens but very few could be found. I believe a lot of people had a chicken dinner that weekend – but not us! The crater

was about thirty feet across. A lot of windows were broken.

Another bomb dropped in Mill Road near Fairview Avenue, but I don't think it went off. It fell through two floors of the house, occupied by the Gorbuts, whom I knew at school.

Alf Evardson

Private Enterprise

At the end of the war, we made a trolley out of old prams parts. We used to go down to Cleethorpes railway station and use our trolleys to carry people's suitcases and bags to their lodgings. There was one official porter on the station and we used to hide in the passage till he went away. Then out came all the trolley lads. We received two or three pence a trip to the lodgings in the Rowston Street area. It was always a good Saturday.

I left school at fourteen and a week later started work at Kirman's Dairy in Mill Road.

Alf Evardson

Mum had the last word

I recall a few houses in Highgate, opposite the old Almshouses in Coronation Road, which were empty at that time and being used to billet soldiers. I used to call and ask the soldier for souvenirs, such as badges. One soldier had a new cap badge. He asked me if we had a bathroom at our house. When I said yes, he said I could have his cap badge if he could have a bath at our house. I raced home and asked my mother. A definite 'No' was the answer. Never mind, I still had my pocketful of shrapnel.

Alf Evardson

Effects of the wars

On 24 February 1916 the whole of Bursar Street School was closed and taken over by the military authorities. The staff and children were transferred to other local schools. In 1917 the military authorities released the school, which reopened on 17 May. Mr Patterson was made temporary headmaster as Mr Kirman had become temporary head of Barcroft. All of Mr Patterson's teachers were women as the men had taken up military service.

Owing to the outbreak of the Second World War, Bursar Street School did not reopen on 4 September 1939 after the summer holidays. The teachers were helping with the evacuation of children to country districts. Many of the children from poor homes had insufficient clothes. Many of the women teachers went to sewing centres at Thrunscoe and Reynolds Street Girls' Schools in order to make clothes for these evacuees.

On 2 May 1941, a bomb exploded in the gardens at the back of the row of houses in Bursar Street facing the infants' school, within fifty yards of the school buildings. Twelve houses were so badly damaged that they had to be demolished. Eighty panes of glass were shattered in the school but all repairs were carried out during the weekend and school resumed as usual on the Monday morning.

From Bursar Street School archives

An ill wind...

The walk from the Lifeboat Hotel to the Winter Gardens in February 1953 didn't take long even in bad weather, but we were aware that it was something more than just a gale

A flooded Bathing Pool after the severe storms of February 1953.

Storm damage to the amusement arcade at the northern end of the Promenade.

The crane used to repair the storm damage was caught by another high tide.

blowing. Once inside we soon forgot the storm until some late arrivals told us of damage and flooding, and that the trolleybuses had stopped running due to flooding in Grimsby Road. On the way home my friend Stuart and I decided we would inspect the damage the next morning.

The first place we visited was Pelham Road in Cleethorpes. I was concerned about the Cleethorpes bus depot, and Stuart wanted to look at Chapman's brick pit where he often fished. After satisfying ourselves they had suffered no damage, we walked on to Fuller Street bridge. We met a very young policeman who was preventing people from using the bridge.

I had my camera hung round my neck, and Stuart had the presence of mind to take his pen and notebook out of his pocket. He always had these handy should a young lady give him her telephone number! The policeman mistook us for members of the press and allowed us to use the bridge.

From there I could see that the railway track had been badly damaged and that gangs had already set about repairing the main line. Between the bridge and the promenade there was a break in the sea wall. All the way along the north promenade, debris was scattered about the roadway and the beach. The amusement arcade on the sands was very badly

Debris littering the railway near Fuller Street bridge.

damaged. One-armed bandits and pintables were scattered across the beach. The pier had stood up to the storm, but some decking had been ripped up and the pay-box was damaged. The brick kiosk the other side of the slipway had a wall ripped away. I had run out of film by now, so we went home for Sunday lunch.

In the afternoon we met several of our friends as usual at the Bathing Pool, only to find that the pool had been flooded and the fence washed away. A pin table was floating in the middle of the pool. We walked along the sea wall and found a large gap in the wall close to the outfall of Buck Beck. At Humberston many of the bungalows at the Fitties had been damaged. Others, although not badly damaged, had been turned on their foundations and were at an angle to the road, and many stayed like that for years to come.

There's a saying about an ill wind that often brings good fortune. For years next to King's Parade promenade there had been mud at the foot of the sea wall, and the Corporation had regularly used a bulldozer to move a sandbank to cover the mud without much success. This storm had done the job for them and piled sand up against the sea wall.

Norman Drewry

9 Transport

Building up the pressure

An elderly employee of the corporation bus undertaking during the 1950s, told me an old legend among transport enthusiasts. We had been discussing the merits of steam lorries over modern internal combustion vehicles. To illustrate his point that steam-powered lorries were not as simple and safe as I had been suggesting, he told this story.

One of the early steam lorries in the area used to ply between Grimsby and Binbrook. The route included the rise up Ashby Hill. This is no obstacle to modern engines, but at the

beginning of the twentieth century it was a notorious hindrance to traffic – both going up and down. First though, you have to understand how steam lorries worked. Water is heated in the boiler by a fire underneath. The steam produced is held by the boiler until it is used in the cylinders. There is no fine control over how much steam is produced, and if too much is generated, the metal of the boiler is apt to give way with a very loud bang. Fragments of metal and scalding steam will fly in all directions, maiming any poor soul who happens to be standing too close. Early boiler designers soon discovered this essential detail,

A strange procession seen on Barnoldby Road, Waltham, in 1996. The red car is being towed.

Trolleybus 58 (FW 8994) emerging from the Pelham Road depot. Notice the concreted lines in the road where the tram tracks had been.

and someone invented the safety valve. The most common one in those far-off years was the Salter Spring safety valve. A cover over a hole in the boiler was held down by a spring that could be adjusted by a screw. Before the pressure reached danger point, the cover would lift and allow excess steam to escape. The advantage with the Salter valve was that it could be adjusted for different types, sizes and strengths of boiler.

The driver of the Binbrook steam lorry knew how his Salter valve worked, and knew of the delay Ashby Hill could cause if he had to stop several times for his boiler pressure to recover. His solution was simple. He screwed down his Salter safety valve for extra pressure to help him up Ashby Hill, sometimes sitting on his engine, perhaps puffing contentedly on his pipe, waiting for the pressure to build up inside the boiler. The elderly employee told me he often wondered about that driver. Did the chap ever give a thought to how strong (or weak!) the metal of his boiler was? Boilers have exploded elsewhere in similar circumstances, but I have not heard of one exploding at the bottom of Ashby Hill. If you have, do tell.

Ray Woods

A change of fortune

The Manchester, Sheffield & Lincolnshire Railway brought visitors and prosperity to the area when the line to Grimsby opened in 1846. The extension to Cleethorpes opened in 1863 but at first was only a single track. At its peak the Grimsby-Cleethorpes line was used to capacity, with Saturday tourist excursions and the fish traffic to and from New Clee sidings. In the 1970s, the track was 'rationalised', which really means cut back to the bare minimum. I suppose we should be grateful that Cleethorpes does retain its line.

The original direct route, with its long straight stretches of level line, ran from Sheffield via Retford and Gainsborough to Barnetby. It is still there, but in 2002 it sees trains only on Saturdays, and then just three passenger workings each way. Occasionally, a diverted freight train may use the route, but again only on a Saturday when the signal boxes are open. The secondary line from Doncaster via Scunthorpe, built piecemeal and twisting along the contour lines, now functions as the 'main line'.

Barry Hall

Celebrating the Coronation

Somebody known to me, although I will not mention his name, celebrated the Coronation of our Queen in 1953 by visiting several public houses in Grimsby's old market place. He then decided to go to Cleethorpes to see if there was any dancing at the Winter Gardens. He remembers getting on a trolleybus but nothing else until a man in overalls said, 'Wake up, mate. You can't sleep here all night.' Our friend found that he had slept for several hours upstairs on the back seat of a trolleybus now in the Cleethorpes depot!

Walking home in the pouring rain, he realised that his raincoat felt very heavy. Feeling in his pockets, he found four blue bags each containing five shillings worth of copper. He must have tendered a pound note for his bus fare, and the kindly conductor got four bags of copper out of his cash box, taking the fare out of one. It saved the conductor having to carry all that weight back to the depot!

John Hewson

'Fares, please!' Jean Ashling's enthusiasm to be a bus conductress was not dampened by patients' toothaches.

'Fares, please!'

As a child I enjoyed the tram journeys with my mother along Grimsby Road towards Riby

Square or towards Cleethorpes. The depot was in Pelham Road near Isaac's Hill and as there were a lot of points nearby, the tram made a lovely clattering noise as it passed over them.

Like most children I loved dressing up. Birthdays and Christmas always ensured that I had a cardboard box, often containing a nurse's uniform or sometimes a fairy outfit consisting of tiara, crepe paper dress fashioned with 'floating panels' and a wand with a magnificent star. Best of all was the tram conductor's outfit, with a flat cap, money bag, ticket holder and a splendid metal device which emitted a strong 'PING' as it punched the ticket. Yes, I was obsessed with 'conducting' and wore out a number of these outfits, so I have been told. Patients visiting my father's dental practice had to have a ticket from me before entering the waiting room. As I had an array of available tickets it must have been a great trial to the poor folk arriving, maybe with violent toothache, to have to undergo 'Fares, please! Where to?' and wait for the correct ticket to be selected and then be punched with a 'PING'!

Jean Ashling

County loses rail link

The railway line from Boston to Grimsby was opened in 1848 by the Great Northern Railway. It served as a direct route to London and as an avoiding line for freight travelling to Scunthorpe from the south.

Dr Beeching felt, however, that its use was limited and ordered its closure. Replacement bus services proved inadequate and short-lived. Passenger trains ceased in October 1970, but a once-a-week goods train kept the Grimsby-Louth section open until late in 1980. The track and ballast were removed with indecent haste.

A group of local enthusiasts decided to open the Grimsby-Louth line as a preservation pro-ject. Circumstances forced them to reduce their goal, but they will soon reach a manageable target of opening the Ludborough to North Thoresby line. It was always planned to be a standard gauge railway, with steam engines pulling coaches.

Now known as The Lincolnshire Wolds Railway, the line received an award from the Heritage Railway Association in 2002 for its good progress after struggling against shortage of funds and volunteers. It ran its first steam train on 28 March 1998, 150 years after the GNR ran its first train on the line.

Barry Hall

House damaged by bus

An incident written about in *Grimsby Remembered* made me recall that I had seen it. I was on my way home from visiting a friend on Clee Road. I walked around the corner to go up Isaac's Hill and stared with astonishment – I could not believe my eyes. There was a double-decker bus parked in the front garden of a house in front of me. Worse still, it had crashed into the front room of the house. I thought there had been some terrible accident and a driver had been taken ill whilst going round the roundabout. But then I realised that buses don't go round that side of the roundabout. So how had this terrible accident happened?

I soon found out when the *Grimsby Telegraph* arrived that night. Apparently a nine-year-old boy had taken the day off school and stolen the bus from outside the depot in Victoria Street. He had then driven it to Isaac's Hill. How he managed the controls amazed me. Fortunately no one in the house was injured, but it was a terrible mess.

Joan East

Isaac's Hill roundabout with Grimsby Road to the left. AEC Bridgemaster number 108 is seen coming down the hill from the High Street, on the number 3 service. These vehicles had unique air suspension which often caused passengers to think the tyres were deflating.

Illuminated trolleybus

During the 1950s, to accompany the end-of-season illuminations at Cleethorpes, one of the trolleybuses was festooned with lights, similar to the style of the Blackpool trams. It was on the route to Grimsby's old market place, but I seem to remember that it travelled only as far as Park Street before returning to the Bathing Pool. Wires had been erected in the side streets so that trolleybuses from either terminus could drive round the block at Park Street, and be facing back the way they had come.

My greatest regret as a child on seeing that 'bus, was that it did not go our way home!

Ray Woods

Cleethorpes seafront bus services

In 1925 the Provincial Tramway Company started a seafront bus service along the promenade at Cleethorpes. It started at the northern end of the promenade and ran along it until it reached the Brighton Street slipway, then joined the Kingsway and terminated at the Bathing Pool. It operated at Easter, Whit Bank Holiday and then weekends until the summer season began, when it ran daily.

The buses used on it were called runabouts and were numbered in a separate series. The fleet numbers were prefixed with the letter R. Two types of buses were used, the first being three Guy toast-racks which had no sides and

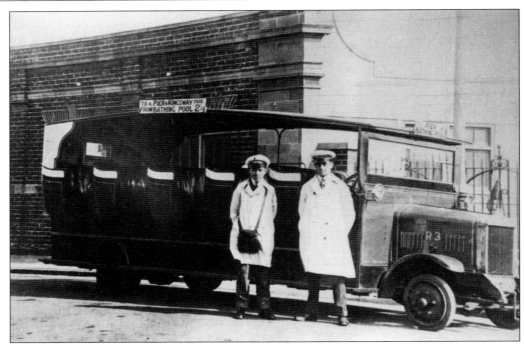

A Guy 'toast-rack' runabout with small, solid wheels, waiting for passengers outside the Bathing Pool. The fare to the pier was 2d.

seats four abreast, very small wheels, some having solid tyres. The second type were six-wheeled Chevrolets, which were normal twenty-seater buses, but with a canvas roof, which in fine weather was folded back.

In 1936, Cleethorpes Corporation bought the tramways and buses from Provincial, and renumbered the Runabout buses into their own series of fleet numbers and repainted them from their original green livery into dark blue and cream.

At the outbreak of the war the service ceased and the buses were scrapped or used as civil defence vehicles. One Chevrolet survived the war to become a lorry for the Parks Department. Cleethorpes Corporation also inherited from Provincial a Guy twenty-seater bus with a canvas top and sometimes used it on the seafront service. During the war it was used by a private bus operator to transport work-

men to and from airfields being built or extended.

Norman Drewry

Post-war seafront services

It wasn't until after the formation of the Grimsby-Cleethorpes Joint Transport Committee that seafront bus services began at Cleethorpes. A minibus based on the Morris J2 van was purchased in 1959. The service began at the North Sea Lane terminus of the No. 12 route, travelled along St Anthony's Bank and circled the Humberston Fitties camp. A similar minibus was added in 1963 but in 1964 the service was replaced when it became possible to operate normal buses along the track beside the Boating Lake and across Buck Beck. The service commenced at the pier, travelled along Alexandra Road, the Kingsway and King's Road. As the camp expanded, the service was extended. Standard single-deck buses were usually allocated to the route but at times an open-top double-decker was used.

John Hewson

Changing the route

I used to watch fascinated as the conductor of a trolleybus changed the route for the trolley poles to take. He would pull a handle dangling at the side of a roadside support pole for the overhead wires. I remember seeing it done at High Cliff for a number 12 to return towards Grimsby. Normally the wires were set for the trolleys to go on to the Bathing Pool. I would

have loved to pull the handle myself, but in those days we were brought up with 'don't touch things that don't concern you'. Once round the circle, the trolleys re-joined the main route without further help. I was interested in trains about the same time, and knew how points worked, which put the wheels of the wagons on to a different track. But these trolley wires carried electricity as well, so that was an extra complication.

Ray Woods

Late night buses

In the early 1950s very few young people had their own transport and were dependent on buses. Normal bus services ceased at 11 p.m. so organisers of dances or the management of

The Joint Transport Undertaking's smallest bus, number 1, seen here with driver/conductor E. Smith in 1959. This Morris J2 ran a public service to the Fitties camp from the roundabout at the end of North Sea Lane. Carrying only eleven passengers, it must often have been full!

dance halls hired buses to take the late-night dancers home. At this time there were two separate Corporation Transport undertakings. Grimsby could cope alone with the Grimsby dance halls, but Grimsby buses had to help out at the Winter Gardens and Café Dansant. The café buses departed from the Bathing Pool but the Winter Gardens, buses lined up outside the entrance. It was more convenient for the café dancers to get on the Winter Garden's buses. As the management were responsible for any loss incurred operating the buses, the café owners were most upset that their patrons were not using their buses. Eventually the two manage-

Cleethorpes trolleybus 54, looking as good as new, on display at Sandtoft Transport Centre in 2000.

JV 8733 (Guy Arab number 79) at High Cliff about 1960. Keen-eyed locals will spot that the destination blind is incorrect. The vehicle behind is number 42, one of six STL types bought secondhand from London Transport. Notice the handle hanging at the side of the bus stop pole, used to change the route of the trolley wires above.

ments came to an agreement and hired one set of buses between them. The buses used were both motor and trolleybuses, and they followed mainly the daytime routes. Several buses would travel the No. 6 route via Clee Road and Weelsby Road to Fryston Corner then take up the No. 9 route to Fairfield or the 3A route to Bradley Cross Roads. The fare was 6d providing you did not cross the town boundaries – then the fare doubled.

Having taken a girl home from a dance, a boy could have a long walk home. A Cleethorpes boy took a girl home to Nunsthorpe and was fortunate to be friendly with the conductor and got a lift back to the Cleethorpes' depot. My friend Dave asked to see a girl home and was shocked to find out

that she lived in a Wolds' village. After he tried to work out which was nearer – Fairfield or Bradley Cross Roads – she told him that she was staying with her friend in Cleethorpes. He still had a long walk home to the Yarborough Road area. At least he had company for part of the way home because the friend she was staying with was my current girlfriend.

Norman Drewry

Trolleybuses live on

On page 41 of *Grimsby Remembered* is a photograph of three redundant local trolleybuses in a Grimsby scrapyard. The middle one was number 54 (FW 8990) of the Cleethorpes

Trolleybus 64 (HBE 542) at the Bathing Pool. It was the second of a pair bought new in 1951. Number 63 was scrapped in 1995 after preservation attempts failed.

fleet. Sold for scrap in 1958, number 54 was bought for preservation in 1968, though its condition was poor. In removing it from the scrap line the other two vehicles were badly damaged. It had several homes before being moved to Sandtoft Transport Centre and in 1981 was purchased by Andrew Fieldsend. Many serious problems have been overcome since and the vehicle now looks much as it did when new in 1937. Andrew looks forward to seeing 54 in service at Sandtoft, but would really like to see it posed outside the former depot in Pelham Road, or even parked next to the surviving traction pole at the former Bathing Pool terminus, 'recreating a scene that was so familiar to many people almost half a century ago'.

None of Grimsby's trolleybuses survived beyond withdrawal, but two more of the Cleethorpes fleet did. Number 59 was used in Walsall after its home system closed. From there, it too went to Sandtoft, where it is in a poor state. Number 63 also found its way eventually to Sandtoft in 1990, but it was then moved to Birmingham for restoration. In 1995 it was sold and scrapped.

Barry Hall

Changing the names

Starting as a steam railway in 1948, the miniature railway became electric in 1954, returning to steam in 1973. The railway was owned by the council between 1951 and 1991, and is now owned by the Cleethorpes Coast Light Railway Ltd. It was the only 14¼ inch narrow gauge railway in the country.

It had a number of stations over the years, having been extended in 1973. Its engines were number 800 *Rio Grande*, and 1492 *Konigswinter*, after Cleethorpes' twin town in Germany.

Cleethorpes Town station opened 1948. It became the Bathing Pool in 1978 and Kingsway in 1991. At the other end of the line was Thrunscoe station in 1948, which became Lakeside in 1991, but was closed due to vandalism in 1992. By this time it was only part way along, as the line had been extended.

Zoo station was the end of the extended line and opened in 1973. It was renamed Leisure Park in 1978, Witts End in 1991, Meridian in 1992, and then Lakeside in 2000. This today is the Brief Encounters tea room, reminiscent of the film which was made on Carnforth station.

The original journey took five minutes in 1970 (Thrunscoe to Cleethorpes Town), eight minutes on the extended line in 1973, and still seven or nine minutes in 1993 and 2000.

Lester Kitching

Watching the trippers' trains

After the Second World War, I often went behind Hawkey's fish restaurant on the promenade to watch the steam engines being turned ready to take the day-tripper excursion trains back. The coaches of the trains were stored at New Clee sidings. Coaches and sidings in those days were nearly always full.

David Bradley

New must be better ...?

The Grimsby-Immingham Electric Light Railway had been built in 1912 to carry Grimsby men to work at the new docks opened that year at Immingham. By the late 1950s the tramcars were worn out, the track needed replacing, and the system was seen as

One of the steam engines is prepared for service on the miniature railway near to the Boating Lake. At this time the track gauge was unique at 14¼ inches. This was a result of the contractors measuring between the centres of the rails instead of between the inside edges. The gauge should have been the standard 15 inches.

On the last day of operation, 1 July 1961, trams muster at the Immingham terminus ready to depart to Grimsby on their final journey. Most were destined for the scrapyard, and the two towns lost a fast, direct (if somewhat uncomfortable) service.

old-fashioned and useless. The last day of operation was set for Saturday 1 July 1961.

David and I decided to have one last ride to Immingham and back, and joined the hundreds of others bidding farewell to the line. Many extra trams were run, and it was a pleasant, if sad, day.

What no one could convince us of was the logic of replacing such a fast and efficient form of transport with a bus service that travelled twice as far, took over twice as long, and cost twice as much. Was that progress?

Barry Hall

New Waltham bus services

Cleethorpes service number 4 used to come along Peaks Lane, turning round at Station Road. It often returned to Cleethorpes via North Sea Lane. It ran just a few times each day. The Grimsby service number 8 ran from Humberston through New Waltham to Grimsby town centre. Grimsby service 9 went from Old Waltham to the town centre.

Revd Roy Allison

The Lincolnshire Coast Light Railway

This railway was run by a small private company and existed in Humberston from 1960 to 1986. It was narrow gauge and one mile long.

Its stations were North Sea Lane (1960) and Beach (1960), St Anthony's Bank (1966) and South Sea Lane (1966).

On the journeys that I made behind the 1903 0-4-0ST engine *Jurassic*, it took five minutes (1970, 1973 and 1978) and on each occasion was non-stop. I don't know how often the two intermediate stations were used.

Lester Kitching

Cleethorpes Market Place in around 1960, with a variety of public service vehicles, including a Nottingham Corporation double-decker. Steel's well-known fish restaurant is on the right.

The type of railway engine that was the most common in this part of the country during the post-war years. This simple, basic design was put together in 1942 by LNER. Chief Mechanical Engineer was Edward Thompson. The Class B1 was a 'maid-of-all-work' to be seen on fast passenger workings to London King's Cross, local passenger trains to New Holland, and fast fish trains to various destinations. Here, number 61126 passes under Fuller Street pedestrian bridge in the early 1950s. Many drivers admired their strength, but admitted they gave the crew a rough ride.

Drama on the trams

One dark and foggy evening in the 1930s, a late-night tram pulled up at the terminus near the Bathing Pool. It was so miserable that the driver decided to wait a while before turning his trolley arm around to collect current from the Grimsby-bound overhead wire. He sat down in the relative warmth inside the tram and became engrossed in conversation with his conductor.

Suddenly he jumped up after realising that they should be on their way. He grabbed his control handle and rushed to the driving position at the Grimsby end, and soon they were moving.

As his tram rounded High Cliff, the driver watched another proceeding towards the Bathing Pool. Just when the two passed he saw the other's lights go out, and he knew what that meant. The other tram's trolley had come off the overhead wire, and the crew would have to struggle in the dark and wet to replace it. He thought no more about it and continued on his way.

They passed another tram at the top of Isaac's Hill, and it too was suddenly plunged into darkness as the vehicles passed. Our driver again felt pity for the crew, and was wondering about this unusual coincidence, when there was a loud bang above. His tram was likewise plunged into darkness, and ground to an abrupt halt. He leapt out on to the road to discover that his conversation at the Bathing Pool had cost him dearly.

Between the Bathing Pool and the bottom of Isaac's Hill, the overhead wires were supported on poles at the sides of the road. At the bottom of Isaac's Hill, the support poles were placed in the centre of the road. His trolley arm, that he had forgotten to turn, had been pushed in front of his tram on the wrong wire. Consequently it had knocked off the trolleys of the two trams it had passed, his own trolley arm hitting the central support caused the loud bang.

The story goes that the driver received a ticking off but did retain his job.

And who says trams are boring?

Barry Hall

5395b

Looking from High Cliff along Alexandra Road. This postcard was sent to Mr Frith of 86 Milton Road in Fleetwood. Unfortunately the stamp and franking date have been removed.